NarcTurnal

Kay D Johnson

Johnson, Kay D
Narcturnal

ISBN 978-1-989382-04-2 (pbk.)

ONE

Detective Richard Wallace marched into Captain Bird's office with his fists clenched and arms flailing. He stomped his feet squarely in front of his desk and yelled, "A stakeout. There's no Goddamn way I'm going on any stakeout. I'm head Detective. Christ, I thought I was finished with these pissy ass jobs." He sidestepped from one end of the desk to the other, angrily glaring into his Captain's in the face. He bellowed again, "A stakeout. A God damned stakeout." Suddenly he stopped dead, sweetly grinned at the man behind the desk and waved with wiggling fingers, "Hi ya, Birdy. Buddy, old pal."

"Real funny, asshole." Birdy stood up, so he could look his underling straight in the eye. "It's a drug deal thing. It's just one more," Captain Bird peered over the top of his thick glasses, smiled, and rubbed it back in his face. "And since you are the Head Dick around here, you should be honored." Seeing that his compliment didn't impress his Detective, he added, "Look, everybody else is tied up with other cases and you're free. That's all. Besides Brogan here would feel so lonely without you." With his almost double chin, Birdy pointed to the man sitting in the chair against the wall, half-hidden behind the opened door.

1

"Hi ya, Dick Head." Detective Brogan Kellar was sitting with his arms crossed and smiling wildly. His green Irish eyes immediately lit up with friendship when Richard turned around. Then his face reddened as he realized that the awkwardness between them might still be there. He wondered if Richard had forgiven him by now? Or did he still hold hostility toward Brogan?

After a quiet pause, a smile slipped across Richard's face. "Holy shit! You stupid bastard! How ya been?" Richard stuck out his massive hand.

Brogan jumped to his feet. "Not bad. Well, that is, until I was told I had to go on a stakeout with you, dog face." He shook Richard's hand firmly.

He had missed his friend.

"Christ, eight hours cramped up in a smelly van with you. I must have done something really wrong in my last life to deserve this kinda shit again."

Inside, Brogan hoped he was teasing, so he joked back, "Love you too, Dick Head."

Birdy cleared his throat, "Okay you two, enough reminiscing. Sit down and shut up. Some of us around here actually do work and enforce the law." They sat down as he pulled a crinkled red folder from the top shelf of the filing rack. "You'll love this assignment. Easy as pie. All you two morons have to do is sit in the van, tape some conversations, and munch on doughnuts. Simple as syrup."

"Yeah. We've heard that before. Remember the Sealey case? That one was easy as pie too." He looked at Richard sideways, "So did that scar of yours ever fade? How many stitches was it, twelve or seventeen? I always get it mixed up."

"Twenty-two." He went to pull up his shirt but Brogan stopped him.

"Shit, not again with the scar crap. Yeah, you took a knife swipe to the ribs. So what? You wanna see my scars?" His eyes had that boyish twinkle he was famous for.

Birdy interrupted, "Anyway. This one's simple. No footwork involved. Great for you old farts. Just a little phone bugging and some camera surveillance. And if the perp shows up, call it in. We'll pick him up when he's gone from the booth. He might be watched and we don't want anyone to suspect that he's been arrested. So, we don't even want you to leave the van when he shows up."

"I can handle that. But what exactly are we hunting for, Birdy?" Only Richard could call the Captain by that nickname. They started out in boot camp together and quickly became best buddies. Birdy was the first Blackman Richard had ever known personally. Over the past twenty years they worked, on and off, in the same precinct. They respected each other's choices of positions within the department. Birdy wanted to be Captain, to be in charge of it all—despite its stresses and headaches. Richard, on the other hand, needed to physically work on the streets. That's where he believed he accomplished his best work and where he provided the best possible protection for the community he lived in.

He was born a street cop.

"Two nights back, the 'Hot Tip' phone line got an anonymous call about a drug deal that's supposed to go down on Friday morning. A large shipment of crack cocaine. The informant said that someone was going to call the buyer in the next couple of days to set up the drop-off. We want that caller. He's our ticket to the information we need to bust the rest of them. This time we're going after the big guys." Birdy opened the file and scanned its pages, "According to this, the call's gonna be made from a payphone located on the corner of Bridge and Pine."

"That's down by the lawyer's block." Brogan was familiar with that part of town. He had grown up in the Irish tenements, ten blocks over from Bridge Street.

"Three-piece suiters. Hey, you still lust after the ladies in those uptight tweeds?" Richard slapped him on back. Brogan's brown leather jacket made the slap sound harder than the hit really was. "You still got that thing for high heel shoes?"

Brogan thought, 'How he'd know?' Knowing that someone else might know his fetish made Brogan squirm nervously in his seat. He covered up his worried expression with a he-man remark. "Yep. Shorts skirts, long legs, and stiletto high heels. Damn sexy stuff." He took the heat off himself by turned the tables back on Richard. "You still got a thing for sexy blondes?"

"Damn right. That's why a married one. You remember Sally?"

"Oh yeah...Sally." Brogan put on his dirtiest grin, "She still got those long sexy legs of hers?" Richard had a slight jealousy problem when it came to his wife and other men looking at her. Brogan remembered that fact and thoroughly enjoyed watching Richard get all worked up over it.

He fired Brogan a nasty look. "Hey, get your own girl, asshole"

Exasperated, Birdy cut in. "Are you two just about done?" He had been reading the job schedule of the stakeout. "Henderson and Forman are on the shift before you. They are..."

"Oh, fuck no! Not Funky Forman," Brogan groaned. "Man. That guy will stink up the whole place." By the look on Birdy's face, some explaining was necessary. "Forman's on this garlic kick. Eats tons of the shit. Raw garlic buds by the hand full. Some kinda homeopathic mambo jumbo. He says it helps purify and clean his blood." He pointed to his own face. "Cleans my God damned nostrils out. That's what it does. Christ, he works on the first floor and I swear I can smell that stinky bastard up on the third floor. He reeks of the shit." He pinched his nose and scrunched up his face to emphasize his disgust.

In a faint voice, Richard used his best Italian accent, "Salami. Lots a salami."

Brogan burst out laughing. "Holy crap! I'd forgotten about that." Richard joined him in the laughter. "Salami. That's still funny."

Birdy plopped down in the chair behind his desk. "This reminiscing of yours is gonna take a while, isn't it?" He knew when to give up.

Brogan got serious, "Nah. It's almost shift change. Henderson's cool. Friendly guy. Likes baseball. I worked with him on the Cassidy Embezzlement case. Very organized." In his chair, he shifted from one cheek to the other cheek, "And ... well ... he doesn't stink."

Richard spit out a laugh. The two of them started giggling like schoolgirls again.

Birdy lost it. "That's it! Shut the fuck up and listen. Both of you. The cars waiting outside the motor pool. It's the old grey sedan. Be at the van for shift change at 5:30, that'll give the guys time to fill you in and get back here by 5:45 to finish their paperwork." Looking directly at Richard. "And no bullshit this time. You hear me?"

With a genuinely innocent expression, he batted his eyes and sweetly smiled at the Captain. "Who? Little ole me?"

Birdy slammed down the file as he yelled, "Yeah you, Dick Head. No bullshit this time. That's an order. You got it?" Birdy's face started to turn deep red, signaling that his blood pressure was creeping up on him and he had finally reached his limit of their stupidity.

Richard changed into a disciplined police officer he was within seconds. He sat up straight in his chair. It was time to get serious. "Yes, Sir. Understood, Sir."

The Captain handed each officer his copy of the report. Looking over the top of his black-framed glasses, he spoke steadfast, "Keep it clean and for Christ sakes, keep awake. I want a full report on my desk first thing in the morning." The last statement was aimed directly at Brogan. By the creases in Birdy's face, the Captain was clearly agitated now.

Brogan knew it too. He answered fast and appropriate. "Yes, Captain."

"That will be all." Then he truly dismissed them, by turning his back on them to looking out the window. They both understood the unspoken message immediately.

Brogan was the first one to scurry out of the Captain's office with Richard quickly following right behind him. Down the hall, they heard Birdy shut his door, sol dly.

He stopped Richard at the too of the stairwell. "Jesus. What the hell did you do? I haven't seen him get that pissed off since...well, come to think of it, I don't ever remember him getting that pissed. And so quickly. What ya do Richie-boy?"

Richard's face drained pale. He changed the subject fast, "Look at the time. We better get going if we want to relieve the guys on time," Richard headed down the stairs. "You got everything you need or do you need to stop by your locker?"

"Nope, I'm good." He noticed that Richard dodge his question but decided to leave it alone. Richard was still standoffish toward him and he didn't want to push it. He would have to ask all his questions later in the shift. Mostly, he wanted an answer to the one question that had been bothering him for so long—Why?

On the car ride downtown, they only discussed the information in the file. No personal conversation. Just business. The awkwardness hung tensely in the air. By the time they arrived at the stakeout site, they were completely familiarized with the case.

They followed the normal stakeout procedures as mandated by police protocol. Richard parked the car across the street from the van so that Forman and Henderson could see them on the monitor. Brogan was the first to leave the unmarked cop car. He casually walked to the surveillance van, depicting himself as Joe Average out for a stroll. When he reached the van, he slipped into the side sliding door that Henderson held ajar for him. Richard waited the allotted ten-minute interval and repeated the same systematic process.

"Hey, Dick Head. Took you long enough." Dick Head was Richard's nickname and Henderson liked uses it as much as possible. "Did you lose your way? Dick Head."

And Richard always shot back. It was their little game. "Such wit. It must have taken you all shift to figure that out." The air in the van was thick with the smell of sweat, coffee, and raw garlic.

Forman was loud and blunt. "Okay, here's the deal. It's 5:43. We're heading to the station so we can put in our reports." He waved the already completed reports over his head. "Tonight, I wanna be home by 6:30 so I can have supper with the old lady, yak with the kids, and be sitting in my big fat easy chair by 7:15. For once, just once, I'd like to watch an entire fuckin' baseball game without somebody buggin' the shit out of me."

"Christ, I hear ya there." Henderson had twin teenage daughters with lives that were always in some kind of crisis and to him, those disasters only seemed to happen when his favorite sporting events were on television.

"Dandy. Then listen up Dick Head. The Perp hasn't shown up yet and it's been one fuckin' long boring day. You know the kind, 'Bring home milk, bread and frozen broccoli'. Mostly domestic crap."

"The drunk with the blue Mohawk was kinda funny," Henderson winked at Forman, "but nothing great happened."

"Brogan will fill you in on the rest of the info crap. I'm out of here." Forman grabbed his duffle bag and headed for the partially open door.

Richard stopped him. "Wait, wait. I got a joke for ya."

"Oh fuck, a Richie joke." Forman despised his stupid jokes.

"Did you hear about the mob boss who went to a cherry farm and bought a bing?" Brogan and Henderson groaned.

Forman tilted his head sideways, "I don't get it." That's why Forman hated Richard's jokes.

"Shit." Henderson covered his face with his hands. Peeking through his fingers he growled, "I'll explain t to you when I get to the car." He shoved Forman out the open door and rammed it closed behind him. "Yep, one really long day." With buffed cheeks and pinched nose, they understood what he meant right away. On the monitor, they watched Forman walk toward the sedan. Halfway across the street, he started laughing, turned toward the van and gave the guys the thumbs up. He finally got it.

"What a fuckin' moron. So much for being undercover. I swear that asshole is determined to get me killed. And each day he slowly does a bit more destruction," he blew out his stress, "No wait. I'm sure he's contrived a diabolical plan to annoy me to death."

They all laughed. Yet Brogan wasn't sure if Henderson was truly joking. He knew first hand that working with Forman could be an incredibly frustrating ordeal. There was no question that Forman was an excellent police officer—the real problem was his personality. At one point or another, Forman had worked with everyone on the force and no one could stand him as their partner. Most begged Birdy for a 'mercy transfer' within the first two weeks of being Forman's partner.

"Well, at least now I don't have to explain it to the idiot." After the 'okay it's clear' from Richard, Henderson left for the sedan. "See you guys later."

When he was gone, Richard opened the passenger door windows and turned on the vent. "You're right, he does stink."

Brogan laughed hard. "Told you so."

He looked up through his eyebrows at him, "Still a smart ass, I see."

In the monitor, they watched the guys pull away. As if on cue, Forman honked the horn and waved at the van. Henderson hit him on the side of the head with his paperwork. Richard shook his head, "I'm sure glad you're my partner." Brogan felt encouraged by his remark. Maybe tonight they would be able to talk it out and repair their damaged partnership...and hopefully their friendship.

It seemed like they were in some kind of reversed time warp. Although they hadn't worked together in over four years, everything was predictably the same. Richard sat at the back of the van, preparing to operate the audio/recording equipment. As always, his officer's logbook was placed by his right hand and coffee mug on his left. Brogan sat in front of the control panels near the large side van window. Surveillance cameras were his specialty. With a kind of magical knowledge that only he possessed, he could work any type of camera the police force gave him. Even the old crappy ones that many other officers had long ago deserted. Onsite camera repairs were so common for him that he began to bring his own tools from home so he could work on them immediately.

His true talent was the way he maneuvered the cameras. One boring July afternoon, Brogan bet Richard that he could read the year of a dime someone had dropped on the sidewalk clear across the street. It took him two and a half minutes of adjusting and Viola! there it was in Technicolor on the monitor, 1961. That was the easiest twenty bucks Brogan ever made off Richard.

"One fresh tape." Richard slipped in the tape marked SHIFT 4/#11 into the machine's slot. He put the last shift's tape into the surveillance team's carrying case. He wiggled his butt in the chair until it felt comfortable. He poured himself a coffee from his thermos and in his best Yogi the Bear voice yelled, "And let the games begin."

Brogan shook his head. To him, Richard hadn't changed one damned bit.

TWO

The stakeout was located on an oddly shaped intersection. Bridge Street was a two-lane roadway running west to east. Pine Lane, a one way, approached it on a 30-degree angle from the southeast. The phone booth itself was in front of the small office building located in the middle of the fork.

On the south side of Bridge Street, the van was parked in the middle of three parking spaces that the police had sectioned off with orange construction cones. The van itself was on an angle across the space facing toward Pine Lane. It wasn't a perfect view for the officers but it was the best spot available on such a peculiar corner.

As Brogan did a sweep with the camera, they analyzed the street across from the van. Directly opposite them was a five-story office building. Its front was all black glass that reflected the surrounding street. In it was the mirror image of the surveillance van, deep burgundy and on its door were the words, 'Peter's Plumbing, Industrial/Commercial/Residential, 1-800-FIX-PIPE, 24 Hrs Service.' In between flashes of passing cars, Brogan focussed the camera on the building's nameplate. The gold colored letters were worn and hard to read. Hamish, Roberts, and Wilkinson - Attorneys.

To its left was a diner called SPOONS. Its drab faded-green exterior was lit by long fluorescent lights, one continually flickered on the old English style woodwork. Inside was a large counter with stools along its front. The typical coffee paraphernalia lined the wall behind it. It was obviously a family restaurant, its dining area of seven small tables, each one covered with a red checked tablecloth and a tiny bunch of silk yellow flowers in its center. Beside the coffee shop was a narrow alleyway that led to nowhere of concern. Passed the alley were other sombre brick office buildings.

To the right of the lawyer's building was a high-end clothing store that was closed for the evening. In the window stood three female manikins displaying their fall collection of business suits. Brogan scanned them from top to bottom with the camera. Mentally, he noted that they had no shoes on. It disappointed him. The name 'Suits You Fine' was scribed in heavy white calligraphy across the glass of the front window.

A doorway to a top floor apartment created a transition between the two architectural styles. Beside that doorway was a small, narrow, pizza place. The entrance to 'Tony's Pizzeria' was on its left and a huge picture window spanned the rest of its front. Above it was a modestly hand-painted sign. From across the street, the officers could see behind the long perpendicular counter and straight through to the busy kitchen. The man sitting on one of its red stools was talking on the phone. His features were clearly Italian, so they assumed that it was Tony himself. There were no tables, just four stools at the counter, indicating it was take-out only. Beyond Tony's were more lifeless office buildings.

A woman dressed in a blush pink business suit made her way through the busy early evening traffic.

"Look, its Miss Pink Pants." Richard was already getting bored. When Richard got bored, everybody was a target for his sharp-pointed tongue. Brogan ignored him and focussed the camera on her. He scanned her, starting at her head and worked his way down her body. For a long moment, he paused the camera so that her legs and feet were both centered on the screen.

Richard reverted to his childhood by sneezing and barking 'Pervert!' at the same time.

Brogan knew he was only teasing but concealed his fetish again with yet another macho comment. "Whoa, nice gams! Wouldn't you like to slide yourself between those long silky beauties?"

"You really are one sick fuck, aren't you?"

Brogan only laughed, mostly because Richard didn't know how much of a 'pervert' he truly was. He had kept his fetish a secret for years. His wife enjoyed the same fetish, which made it even more arousing. She had the best collection of hand-made Italian leather shoes and silk stockings a cop's salary could buy.

He missed her.

Richard didn't say much—he was busy pondering. Something was bothering him about those images on the screen. Her legs, her shoes, her feet...BAM! That's when it hit him—The Feet! Brogan had focussed most of the camera's shot on her brown suede shoes. Brogan Kellar was a 'Foot Fella.' In all the years that he had known Brogan, his past friend, and partner, he hadn't noticed this aspect of him. In the back of his mind, he recalled reading about the origins of his friend's first names in one of his daughter's baby name books. Ironically the name Brogan was Gaelic for 'brog', which translated into the English word 'shoe'. A foot fetish. Now he really wondered about Brogan and his very private life. From the corner of his eye, he scrutinized his partner closely yet kept his thoughts to himself.

Her long dark brown hair streamed behind her as she jumped onto the sidewalk avoiding a car that nearly hit her. She reached into her matching brown purse for the quarter she had put there the night before. She knew she was going to call him tonight and wanted to be sure she had the right change. She slowed down her pace as she began to think. What was she going to tell him this time? She was working late again, that's all, the same excuse as last time. 'No big deal' she convinced herself. When she got to the phone booth, she stopped to take in a deep breath, calming her nerves. She braced herself for what she was going to do next. She was going to lie to her husband—again. Then the image of 'him' popped into her head. Opening the booth's door, she had decided what she was going to say and how she was going to say it.

She slipped in the quarter and punched her home number. It rang, Once...twice...

"Hello?" a male voice answered.
"Hi! It's me. What'cha you doing?"

"Making salad. Tonight, it's baked chicken with orange fennel salad ... all your favorites." He paused and waited for it. Silence on the other end always meant the same thing.

"Sorry baby, I'm working late tonight." She bit her lower lip, stopping her herself from blurting out words that would reveal she was deceiving him. Too many given details would expose the fact she was spinning a lie.

"What? Again? That's three nights this week." He was trying his best to not get angry. He reminded himself that she loved her work and was extremely talented at it. He tried hard not to pressure her about the amount of time spend at the office. After all, she had done the same for him when he was working his way up the ladder in his chosen career. He would have to bite his tongue again tonight. He would do it for her.

"I know! I know! Bruce is a major asshole! What can I say? He's my boss. I have no choice." She let out a loud sigh hoping it would emphasize her false disappointment. "I'm really sorry, Sweetheart."

"When's that jerk gonna hire more staff? He's working you too hard."

"The contracts are getting bigger, that's all. They take longer to complete than they used to. It's a very good sign. It means the business is growing. He needs me."

"I wouldn't mind so much if the cheap prick paid you for the extra hours. Salary? What a crock of shit that is." Oops, he was letting his anger slip into his voice again. 'Calm down', he told himself.

"Yeah." She didn't care what he saying, she was looking down at her watch and it was almost seven o'clock. Mentally she yelled at him, 'Get off the damn phone.'

"Oh well, can't be helped I guess." He lowered his voice and calmed himself down again, "So what time do you think you'll be home?"

"Shouldn't take longer than say...ten o'clock?"

"Ten o'clock!" It came out angry, "Oops, I'm sorry. I didn't mean it that way. Ten o'clock, that late again?" He knew that didn't sound right either.

"Yeah." She tried to make the word sound apologetic over the phone.

Hearing the emotion in her voice and knew he had gone too far again. "It's fine. So tonight, it'll be the TV and me. There's a baseball game on tonight and you know I love my baseball. That'll keep me busy." He kept his voice light this time, reminding himself to not add extra pressure to his wife's need to work overtime.

"I'm sorry about this," she paused for effect. She hated having to make up feeble excuses to go with her lies, "The deadline is midnight tonight, west coast time. Hopefully, we should be out of the office by...say...ten o'clock, so I should be home by...ten thirty, eleven at the latest." Nervously, she flipped her hair over her shoulder, scheming was stressful work.

"That late, huh?" His voice echoed his feelings of being let down.

"Yeah, I'm so sorry." She forced disappointment into her voice too. She had to make it sound like she gave a damn, when in fact she didn't care at all.

"I'll try to stay up for you but no promises."

She tried to keep it light, "Yeah, right! So do you want me to wake you up or shall I just leave you on the couch and cover you up like last time?" She always snorted through her nose when she teased him.

"Ha, ha. Funny chick!" he snickered back. "Sorry but five-thirty in the morning comes early for me. I'm usually in bed by nine o'clock. You know that?"

That's what she hated most about him. His stupid sensible routines. His stupid corporate job that dictated his stupid boring life. "Yeah, I know. Listen, I hate to cut this short but I should get back to the office before Bruce messes up something else that takes me twice as long to finish this project."

"Yeah, like last time. What a dick." He despised her boss. Bruce had kept his wife late at the office too many times, cleaning up his mistakes or beating some impossible deadlines.

"Don't remind me. Anyway, I'll see you when I get home."

"Okay. Miss ya. Love ya." He sounded as though he really did miss her.

"Yeah. Love you too, bye." She hung up. The phone line buzzed silent. She hoped she sounded convincing enough that he wouldn't ask too many questions later. She slipped her hand into her jacket pocket and pulled out another quarter. She held it in her palm and stared at it.

"What's she doing?"

"Damned if I know? She's just standing there looking at her hand." Richard sounded bored.

As she bounced the quarter in her hand, her heart began to race. Should she or shouldn't she?

Brogan joked. "I think she's thinking."

She held it between her fingers and studied it for a bit longer. Shrugging her shoulder, she finally put the coin into the phone's slot. A smile formed on her glossy pink lips as she punched the buttons.

It rang. One...two...three...four...she tapped her two fingers on the receiver. "Shit! Pick up! Come on, pick up!" ...five...six...

"Hello?" This man's voice was much deeper than the first.

"Hi! It's me. What are you doing?"

"That's the same question she asked her husband. What's she doing?" Richard shook his head. "Can't be?"

"Shut up! I can't hear her." Brogan squinted his eyes to hear better.

"Well, hello Me! How are things tonight, Me?" The man teased and laughed.

"Ha! Ha! Funny guy!" Her voice was flirtatious, her head held high with a smile on her lips.

Brogan and Richard glanced at each other.

"Waiting for a beautiful woman to call me. Are you a beautiful woman?" His words were playful.

"I don't know, am I?" she held her breath. She still wasn't sure of her lover. This was all so new to her. Her heart raced in her chest. Was she beautiful to him?

"You know you are." His voice took on a deep seductive tone, "Are you coming over?"

She moaned the words, "Oh yes, I'm cumming!" This arrangement was so excitingly sinful. The sneakiness of the situation made the sex more intense.

"Baby, you should really wait until you get here before you cum," he purred out the last word. "Hurry! I'm waiting for my beautiful woman to cum." That final statement made her catch her breath.

"Well, I'll be damned. It looks like Little Miss Pink Pants is actually Little Miss Hot Pants." Richard was the wizard of wisecracks tonight.

"Shut up, will yeah? Man. I've gotta hear this. It just gets hotter and hotter." Brogan was grinning now.

"I'll be there in twenty minutes. Do you have any ice cream or should I bring my own?" Her mouth watered at the memory of their last encounter.

"I've got some leftover from last time. Today, in my imagination I had you looking sinfully delicious. Your hard nipples covered with chocolate sauce waiting for me to lick it off. But right now, my tongue tells me that you'd taste better than chocolate." He made a licking sucking sound.

She gasped and squeaked out, "Make that fifteen minutes." Her pulse pound in her ears, "I've been thinking of ice cream and you. Yummy ice cream … yummy you." She paused for impact, "Fifteen minutes." She sighed out a long sultry, "Bye."

They heard the click. She stood in front of the phone with her hand still holding the receiver. She closed her eyes and visualized their unrestrained sex acts. It had been two evenings past but she could still feel the sensations of it all. Her hot skin...the cold ice cream... his tongue...his fingers...

"Ma'am, Ma'am. Are you done with the phone? Can I use it now?"

She reacted with a tiny squeal and a startled jumped. Her mind was so deep into her fantasy that she hadn't heard him arrive outside the booth.

Behind her stood a young man who seemed to be in a hurry. "I didn't mean to scare you," he blushed as she walked around him. "Sorry, Ma'am. I hope I didn't rush you but I only get fifteen minutes for break."

She recognized him. He was the boy from the coffee shop beside her office. His nametag read, Tommy. "It's all right, I was done anyway." As she walked away, she wondered how long he had been standing there and if he had heard anything she said.

"Here we go again. Ready?"

"Yep! Hope it's as juicy as the last one." Richard had been married for more than twenty years and that last call was the naughtiest thing he had heard in a long time.

The boy watched the lady in pink walk away. 'Ice cream?' he thought. He would have to try that with his girlfriend. He dropped in his quarter and pressed the buttons. Someone picked it up halfway through the first ring, as though they were sitting beside the phone waiting for it to ring.

"Hello?" her high pitch voice squealed in the officer's headphones. Both officers scrunched up their faces with the stabbing ear pain.

"Hi Sugar, it's me."

"Hi Honey! I miss you, kiss, kiss. When is my Pooky Bear coming home?" She squeaked even higher with a pouty Shirley Temple voice. "I hope it's soon. I'm all alone and I need my Honey Man to protect me."

"Ouch! Holy Christ!" Brogan ripped off his headset.

"Oh man, what a voice?" Richard was holding his set as far away from his ears as he could without taking them off. He still needed to hear what was being said by both callers.

"Honey Man? Pooky Bear? I think I'm gonna puke." Brogan shuttered.

"That voice could peel paint," was Richard's only comment. He slowly turned up his volume knob to where he could tolerate her shrieking and still hear Tommy.

"Brandy, I just left four hours ago and you know I have to work until midnight." His voice reflected the contempt he felt for her. She was beautiful. Big green eyes, blonde curly hair and a body that made men stop dead in their tracks. He loved his Brandy but secretly he wished, that with all her beauty, she could learn to be...well...intelligent. At first, the 'dumbness' was kind of cute. Soon he discovered that without a working brain, she lived an empty existence. An existence that depended entirely on him—and that was a lot of pressure. Her dumbness made it impossible for her to get a job, let alone hold onto one. She had become a huge financial burden. She constantly expected the best makeup and newest clothes yet she wasn't capable of earning the money to pay for them. He worked overtime - lots of overtime, to pay for it all. He was tired and stressed out.

"Oh yeah. I forgot. So when are you coming home?"

"Brandy, listen carefully. We are going to the Morgan's tonight for a birthday party. Did you remember to get a present for Derek like I asked you to?" Inside, he already knew the answer.

"Derek's having a birthday? Hurray for Derek!" The image of her bouncing up and down in her chair flashed across his mind. At one time he would've enjoyed watching her bounce

up and down but that titillating thrill had long vanished. Now it only annoyed him.

"Brandy...Brandy! Did you get the present for Derek?" By now he was screaming in the mouthpiece. One, so she could hear him over her torturous squealing. And two, because he was so utterly frustrated with her lack of brains. Anger throbbed in his chest and his head started to hurt.

"Umm, no," She giggled, "I guess I forgot. Sorry, my Honey Man." She giggled again. He had learned to hate that dismissive giggle. Wasn't she smart enough to know that she had let him down again? Hanging his head, he gave up right there and then. Letting out a disappointed sigh, he tried to calm himself. "Don't worry about it. I'll pick up something on the way home. Just be ready at midnight, then we can go straight to the party after I change clothes. Okay?' He heard the receiver hit what sounded like the coffee table. "Brandy? Brandy, are you listening?" On the phone, he could hear the living room floor creaking and her singing.

"We're going to a party! We're going to a party!"

In his head, he cursed, 'Dancing. She's fuckin' dancing.' He tilted his head back to looked toward the sky and grunted. "Fuck me. Somebody, please save me from my life. Kill me...now, right fucking now. Christ, just kill me. Put me out of this misery."

His anger came back. He screamed into the phone. "Brandy!"

Both officers winced with stabbing pains. "My fucking ears." Brogan yanked the headset right off his head this time.

Richard quickly slammed the dial down to zero. "Shit, nobody's that lazy or that stupid. Poor bastard. Why's he putting up with this lazy bitch's crap?" He slowly turned the volume back up. Harsh sounds or not, they had a job to do. Brogan returned his in place, one side hovering over his left ear.

"Brandy! Brandy! Are you there?" He thought to himself 'Stupid bitch'. He yelled again, "Brandy! Are you there?" He heard the receiver scrape across the table as she picked it up again.

"We're going to a party!" More squealing then she suddenly stopped. "Oh, a party. I better start getting ready. I gotta look good for my Honey Man. Bye." Click.

His mouth fell open in disbelief. He slammed down the receiver, "Stupid fucking idiot." Totally overwhelmed with frustrated, he dropped head down. He needed to be honest with himself. "I can't take this shit anymore." He stood there quietly crying, his body shaking with each jagged breath.

Richard was the first to take off his earphones and place them gently on his desk. Brogan let his slide down onto his collarbone. Neither of them could bear to listen to the young man cry. Richard averted his eyes while Brogan planned with the pencil in front of him.

Seeing the booth door open, brogan manned the camera again. "He's leaving."

"Poor bastard." Richard felt sorry for him so he left it at that. No wisecracks. No funny nicknames.

Tommy wiped his eyes with his shirtsleeves and blew his nose on the underside of his apron. Running his fingers through his short-cropped brown hair, he forced himself to stand tall again. The officers sat quietly in the van watching him slowly make his way back to the coffee shop.

Tommy's call left them in a dismal mood. Their own emotions had gone from eroticism to pitiful despair. What could possibly happen next?

Nothing happened.

Not one person went near the booth. The few people that were in the streets walked directly to their cars or made their way down the street to the bus stop. They both sat motionless, watching the world go about its boring everyday business.

Inside the van, the atmosphere turned awkward. So far, Richard and Brogan hadn't been alone together when they weren't busy. The lack of work that previously occupied their time, now created a situation where they had to talk to each other. The silence was straining. Brogan wasn't sure what to say to his once upon a time partner. Should he bring it up now or wait until later in the shift? Out of the corner of his eyes, he watched Richard, hoping to read his mood.

Richard saw his glimpse. "What?"

"Nothing." He squirmed in his seat.

"Got a question for me?"

"No. Why would you ask that?" Brogan wanted Richard to be the first to deal with the touchy subject that lay between them.

"No reason."

The emotional strain between them was heavy. Not only had they been police partners in the past, they had been close personal friends as well. Brogan and his late wife Maeve were the godparents of Richard's youngest daughter, Clare. But now their friendship felt...cumbersome, somehow unnatural. Richard started the small talk. "Baseballs kinda crummy this year. I mean, with all the rain we've had, how are they going to make up the rained-out games? Shit, there must four games that need to be rescheduled."

"Yeah. I had tickets for two of those games and I bet they get rescheduled on the days I work nights."

"That kinda happened to me last spring. My brother-in-law Pat gave me a pair of tickets to a game but my schedule got changed on me and I had to work that night. Lewis's daughter broke her leg slipping off a dock or something stupid like that, so I had to cover his shift. Hey, come to think of it, fucker still owes me for that switch."

Brogan was trying to keep his end of the conversation going. "So what did you do with the tickets?"

"My sister Connie and her jerk boyfriend went instead."

"That was a nice thing to co." The stiffness of the conversation was loosening up a little.

"Not really, I never liked that fuckin' creepy boyfriend of hers. To me, it always felt like he was hiding something. You know the kind? One of those sneaky pricks. Unfortunately, I was right. When my sister found out he had been cheating on her, she fell apart." He stabbed his pen into his note pad, "I could've killed the bastard."

"I hate assholes like that? How did Connie deal with it?" Brogan felt as though Richard's sisters were like his sisters too. He had been involved, one way or another, with Richard's entire families. Brogan and Maeve had gone to all three of his sisters' weddings. He helped Pat find a second job when money got tight for them. He even went ice fishing a couple of times with the Wallace men.

"Well, in true Wallace Style, our sister trashed the jerk's precious red sports car." Pride glowed on his face, "Man, I gotta love that big sister of mine."

"She didn't?"

"Yep. Dana keyed the paint job on the jerk's corvette and the next night, she slashed both front tires. Both misdemeanors of course."

"No hefty charges if she got caught. Smart girl." He wanted all the details, "So um, how'd you find out?"

"Connie told me." He went quiet for a moment. Brogan knew how Richard's mind worked. He was trying to figure out how to say it without getting too mushy. "Dana had confessed to Connie that she was the one who did the dirty deeds and thoroughly enjoyed doing it. Connie came straight to our house after her fight with Dana. We could tell she had been crying, 'cause her eyes were all buffed up and her nose was red. She was in some kinda weird state of shock. Sally told me it was a 'girl thing' and not to worry about it. Sally knows women better than me, so I ignored it. After a shot of my best scotch, she admitted that she felt awful about what Dana had done and wanted to know what she should do about it."

"What did you tell her?"

"Nothing."

"That's not like you. You always give your sisters great advice. That's one of the things they admire about you, you're a fantastic brother."

"No, you idiot. I told her to do nothing. To leave it alone."

"Did she?"

"She did...but I didn't." Richard grinned at him.

"Oh?" He had to hear more. "Continue."

"The jerk came into the precinct all pissed off and yelling like a lunatic about his precious car and demanded to talk to me." He snickered, "That's when it got fun. You see, Birdy already had the heads-up as to what Dana did and Birdy intercepted him before he could get to me."

He sat up straight in his chair. "Birdy? Holy shit."

"Now, you know how Birdy cares about my sisters, right?"

"We all do." He felt he needed to add that, to remind Richard he still cared about him and his people. "A cop's family is every cop's family." In front of his heart, he clasped his two hands together. "The Brotherhood."

"Birdy had him put in one of the interrogation rooms, letting him cool off. Then he came and got me. Christ, it made my day. We left him in there for thirty-five minutes. In the meantime, Birdy ran the jerk's name through the computer. And guess what? Mr. big jerk had nineteen outstanding parking tickets." Richard's grin grew even bigger, "Birdy got Henderson to run off jerk's printouts on the old perforated style computer paper. He double spaced it, making it looked like a really long rap sheet."

"Man, Henderson loves doing that kinda shit. Especially to guys who treat women badly." Brogan did another sweep of the street with the camera. Still nothing.

"Birdy, Lewis, Henderson and me walked into that interrogation room and stood shoulder to shoulder in front of him. The jerk squirmed in his seat like he was a five-year-old and we were his mean old grandmother." Richard swung his chair around, "The jerk's fuckin' eyes grow the sizes of walnuts when Birdy spilled the sheet down onto the table, sheet by sheet. In true Birdy thespian style, all he said was, parking tickets."

"Wish I could've been there. It must've been sweet."

"Oh, that's when the jerk starts stomping around and yelling that it was all fixed and that we were trying to intimidate him. So, Henderson accidentally stepped in the path of his little stomping fit and the jerk plowed right into him."

"How convenient?"

"Lewis cuffed him pronto. He also informed him that he was being charged with assaulting a police officer. And then Birdy, slick as hell, immediately offered him a court-appointed lawyer. That's when the big jerk got very scared and very quiet."

"I bet he did?"

Richard turned to check the monitor again. "We all left the room except for Lewis. He was the one that did the...suggesting."

"Let me guess? If he didn't press charges against Dana, we'd forget about everything that happened. Right?"

"Not quite, we threw in the elimination of his parking tickets as a bonus."

"Ah...how sweet of you guys." Sarcasm, Brogan's friend.

"He took the deal. Oh, and we told him that we'd be keeping the assault charge file handy, just in case he decided to change his mind and required a little refresher. Funniest damned thing happened, the jerk promised that he'd never go near a sister or a daughter of a police officer again." He snorted, "I do believe that he meant it too."

"That's good news for Henderson."

"Yeah, twin teenage daughters. Every Father's nightmare."

Brogan focussed on a woman jogging along the other side of the street. She was wearing orange Converse All-Stars with her red sweat suit. "Christ, it's still dead out there."

"It'll get busy after the dinner hour."

"Speaking of supper. I'm getting hungry. How about you?"

"Umm...I could eat. What's open that close by?"

"Well, we are in the communication slash law district, daytime buildings mostly. Let's see," Brogan rotated the surveillance camera up and down the street. "The pizza joint and the coffee shop are the only things open this time of night."

"No pizza, my guts can't take a whole night of greasy, spicy sauce," Richard massaged his podgy stomach. "What I'd really like is a fresh garden salad or maybe some homemade soup."

Brogan swung around in his chair. "Holy shit! You've sure changed your eating habits. Last time we worked together, you ate hot Italian sausage on a bun with hot peppers and that horrid grainy mustard. What did you call it? A 'grease and fire'."

Richard shrugged his shoulders, "My guts aren't as young as they use to be and my spare tire is getting kinda overinflated. You could use it on a transport by now," He grabbed the flabby band around his waist and jiggled it. "The wife says she wants *us* to get into shape. For retirement, you know, to get healthy. Yep, salad, that sounds good." Brogan had a feeling that it was more than his wife's nagging but he wasn't going to pry. He didn't really want to know that badly and he was positive that bull-headed Richard wouldn't tell him anyway.

"The coffee shop it is. Your turn to buy."

"Fuck you! It is not." Richard Wallace was well known for being the cheapest prick on the force.

"Fuck you, yeah. Look, last time I paid for six of those 'grease and fires', a dozen and half doughnuts and a total of seventeen coffees." He counted the list on his fingers and ended on the large middle one which he held up proudly toward Richard.

"What-ev-er." Richard returned the finger salute.

"Hey, you remember the guy with the sausage cart? With the big black mustache, beady little blue eyes and that big scar that ran from the top of his right cheek down to his Adam's apple. What a scary bastard? Made good sausages though."

"Oh yeah, that ugly shit. Okay, okay, you're right. You did pay last time. Guess I'm buying," he smiled to himself as he pulled the money from his wallet, "But you gotta go get it. Deal?"

"Yeah... sure...whatever." He took the money off Richard's desk and headed out the door.

"Wait..."

"Yeah, yeah I'll get you something healthy," he teased Richard with the word 'healthy'. "Man, just relax." Before Richard could say anymore, he was gone out the door.

Richard followed his partner in the monitor and mumbled to himself, "Fuck, this should be good."

He watched his partner get halfway through the coffee shop when Brogan recognized the boy behind the counter as the boy from the phone booth. He missed a step. He was the only customer in the place and Tommy was patiently waiting behind the counter to take his order, so he had no choice but to order from him. Richard watched them go through the usual motions. He couldn't hear them but he knew the routine. Tommy took the order. When Tommy was giving the order to the kitchen, Brogan turned around and gave Richard the finger. That made Richard chuckle.

As a cop on a stakeout, Brogan took the opportunity to use a real bathroom while he could. The tiny bathroom in the surveillance van wasn't the best size for a full-grown functional man. It left no room for privacy when it came to sounds and smells. When he returned to the counter, they chatted while the order was being made in the kitchen. By the hand gestures, they talked about the weather, baseball scores, and motorcycles. At the end, Brogan got the food and with it, the always-demeaning and pointless, 'Thank you for your business' bull shit. Obviously, Tommy didn't mean it and Brogan couldn't care less. Richard muttered to himself in the van, "Why do they make people say stupid bull shit like that? Who gives a fuck?"

Brogan opened the door. "You son of a bitch! You fuckin' knew he worked there, didn't you?" He threw the top bag at Richard, "You fuckin' prick."

"Hey man, you were sitting right here with me. Weren't ya? Christ, don't get pissed at me 'cause you forgot where he worked. What ya get me?" He opened the paper bag to discover two freshly baked multi-grain buns with no butter on them.

"I got us both some soup. Mine is country chicken noodle … and yours is puree of prick head." He slapped the cardboard carrying tray down in front of grinning Richard.

"Jesus, take a joke, will ya?" The tray held two salads, two bowls of soup, a couple of apples and two large milkshakes, one chocolate, and one strawberry. Instantly, he realized that even after four years of not working together, Brogan still remembered that he like strawberry milkshakes. He had forgotten how much time they had spent cooped up together during those three years of stakeouts. "Looks good." He held up the shake and smiled with his eyes, "Thanks, man."

"Yeah, yeah" he lifted out the salads, "The dressings are low-fat. I didn't know what kind you like these days so I got Tommy-boy there, to give us a bunch of different kinds. But the Italian is mine. Got it?"

"Relax. I'm a French dressing kinda guy anyway." The packet read 'Low fat and Calorie reduced' across the top. Then it dawned on him, no butter. In his mind, he began to add up the peculiar things. Brogan had bought everything low fat, multi-grained and nutritious. No crap, no junky food. In the old days it would have been doughnuts, coffee, and greasy chili fries. Times had truly changed. They both had changed. A fact that disheartened Richard. Neither of them was as young as they used to be and getting older sucked. He took the lid off the soup to let it cool off. Opening the salad container, he howled "You asshole. Alfalfa sprouts. You want me to eat alfalfa sprouts."

"Just try 'em, picky pants. You might even like something new for once."

Richard thought, 'What the hell' and shrugged. He didn't think he would like tofu either and now Sal y cooks it a couple of times a week. He put a fork full in his mouth and chewed. Within seconds he muttered through a mouthful "Holy shit!"

"Oh, come on now, it's not that bad."

"What? No, not that. He nodded towards the monitor, "We've got company and look who it is." On the screen was a familiar face. "Well if it isn't Judge Ethical himself. This should be boring as hell." On when the headsets but they thought they just keep eating, after all, it was only boring Judge Newman.

The dark-haired man in the monitor eyed the streets around him as he stiffly walked toward the booth. He held his briefcase close to his tall body, almost like a shield. He was cautious these days. Death threats made even the most confident man, skittish. Placing the briefcase on the floor, he dug out a nickel and two dimes from the pocket of his pinstriped trousers. He waited until each coin registered in the phone's machinery before putting in the next coin. He visually searched outside the booth again. His hand was shaking as he pushed each number separately and deliberately.

"He even dials a phone anally. Wow, what a surprise?" Brogan's resentment for Judge Newman ran deep. Six years ago, Judge Theodore Newman let a killer go free because the only witness to the murder of a prostitute was another hooker. The Judge decided that the hooker was not a reputable citizen and that her testimony would be of no value to him or the courts. He simply dismissed the case. Brogan had the killer cold, but all the evidence relied on the hooker testimony. Judge Newman threw away 128 man-hours of police work. "Stupid jerk off."

"Shut up. He's done dialing. Listen."

It rings, One...two...three...four...five...
"Yes?"
"I beg forgiveness, Mistress. It is I, slave Ted."
"You dog. You know my orders, speak only when you are spoken to." In the background, they could hear the muffled sound of a male voice.
"Yes, Mistress." Even though she wasn't there in the booth with him, he automatically lowered his head in obedience, "As you command, Mistress. I submit."

Both cops sat up straight at the same time. Richard's eyes grew the size of quarters. "Do you believe this? Holy shit!"

"Shut up, man. Just fuckin' listen." Brogan adjusted the focus on the surveillance camera to get a good picture of the Judge's face.

"That's better. You were ordered to never call here. Never. You know the rules," her authority over him was arousing. "You have disobeyed my orders. You insolent slave,

now you must be punished. Thirty lashes with a bullwhip will teach you. No. A vigorous spanking will correct your memory." She slapped her hand against her leather-bound body to re-enforce her harshness. The hard sound sent an erotic shiver to his groin. Ted sucked in air and held it in with delight. The biting, abusive sound evoked images and sensations. The memory of her fragrance mixed with the scent of hot leather made his nostrils flare. He slid his hand into his right pants pocket. "Never mind, I shall discipline you later tonight, slave. You are not worthy of my time."

All he could think was, 'She dismissed me. I am worthless. I want more. Give me more.' His body bent slightly forward. "Yes, Mistress. As you command."

She snapped, "Silence." Her tone was cold and ruthless, "Ten o'clock tonight. Sharp. Do not be late or there will be a greater hell to pay." She hammered down the receiver.

"Yes, Mistress." In the camera, a perverse smile washed across his face as he closed his eyes. His right hand began to move faster in his pocket. He continued to hold the receiver to his ear so that no one would suspect what he was truly doing. "Yes, Mistress...Yes, Mistress..." He repeated it over and over again.

"Well fuck me! Old 'Holier than thou' is a leather loving, ass sissy," Brogan bellowed. "This is great shit, wait 'til the boys back at the precinct hears about this one," He froze and turned to look at Richard, "Better yet, why don't we ..."

"Already ahead ya there, Bro." Richard was grinning like a mad man. "So, you wanna retire early too?"

"Fuck yeah!" Brogan wriggled in his seat.

"Before the end of this shift, I'll make two...no four...Ah, what the fuck, six copies. That should do it?" Richard could already feel his favorite fishing rod in his hands, "Then I'll erase this section from the main copy, that way nobody else can get to him before us."

"Time Log will be out though." Brogan was always a stickler for details. Looking closer, that's what made him one of the best cops on the force.

"Since when have they ever been right? Besides if I add some extra spaces here and there, no one will ever notice. Camera malfunctions happen all the time. Right?" Richard slapped the desk in front of him. "Thank you, Judge Newman! You old tight assed bastard you."

"Look at him. He's jerking off right there in the booth. Sick fuck," he focussed the camera on his pants to get a clearer shot, "Makes' me wanna puke."

Judge Ted Newman groaned deeply as he finished his business call. He gently returned the receiver to its cradle, picked up his briefcase and left the booth. His right hand never left his pocket. Once again, he visually scanned the neighborhood. When he believed it was safe, he strutted casually to his car and driver that waited for him. Innocently they drove away in his black Lexus with license plate marked PURITY.

The surveillance camera captured every moment.

THREE

Richard went right to work on the tapes. First, he made a copy of the section with the Judge in it. That one he put aside; it was to be re-copied later. Next, he made a copy of the entire original tape but erased the Judge's portions and laid down the occasional static filled gap. That created the malfunction segments. He handed that tape to Brogan.

Brogan, the master of video equipment, adjusted the time log numbers so that they made no sense at all. The clock's digital numbers jumped from larger numbers to smaller numbers than back to larger. He then made a new copy of it and handed that tape back to Richard.

Richard knew that in their Tech Lab they could still pull the images off the original tape even if it was erased. To be on the safe side, he made a copy of the entire manipulated tape and copied it. "There, that should do it."

"Make sure you destroy those other tapes tonight. Don't leave anything behind."

"Destroy my ass. They're all coming home with me. I'm gonna burn them in my BBQ pit except for this beauty." He kissed the tape marked 'CASH #1' with a big smacking sound, "That's one, five more to go." He grinned at Brogan, "Next trip

out, grab some blank tapes. Apparently, these are defective."
He chuckled to himself as he started the procedure.

Brogan sat quietly, watching a man pass by SPOONS
carrying a folded newspaper under his arm, a cigarette dangling
in the corner of his mouth. He waved at Tommy who was bored
and staring out the window. He walked past the lawyer's office
and the suit shop. Again, he waved, this time at Tony who was
sitting reading his newspaper. The cops assumed he must have
been a nice guy from the neighborhood, the way everyone
waved to him. He crossed the street at Tony's and slowly
walked toward the booth with a right-legged limp. He threw
away his smoke before he entered the booth's doors. He
plopped in a quarter and pressed the numbers. He read the
folded length of newspaper while he waited. One ring, two,
three, four, five, six rings…no one answered. He hung up the
receiver. The quarter clanged down through the phone's
machinery. He slipped it out of the cup with his index finger but
it dropped to the floor before he could tuck it in his pocket.
Looking down at the floor, he spotted the gleaming metal disc
in the far corner. He shook his head in disgust. With his hand on
his lower back, he squatted at the knees to pick up the quarter.
He let out a loud groan on his way back up. This time he pushed
the coin deliberately into his pocket with anger.

He left the booth and retraced his path back to SPOONS
where he carefully sat himself down at what looks to be his
favorite table. Tommy automatically brought him a cup of tea
with a little jug of milk. They talked for a moment and Tommy
returned with a piece of cherry pie a la mode. Brogan's mouth

water at the sight of the warm pie and cold ice cream. The man was watching someone out the window and grinned to himself while indulging in his pastry treat.

"We've got a live one. Mean Chick at ten o'clock."
"Ouch! She pissed," Richard snorted.

From the other direction, a young red-headed woman headed straight for the booth. Brogan's camera work detected a pale grey pants suit with patent leather low-heeled pumps. Her steps were forceful strides filled with hostility.

"Crap, where's that stupid quarter? Come on you useless thing?" She was thoroughly stressed out and talking to herself. "Come on. Shit!" Her cloth purse spilled out on the booth floor. "Fuck!" Frantically she fell onto her knees and scattered her items out over the dirty floor not really caring about what happened to any of it. Plucking out a quarter she stood on top of the contents and jammed it into the slot. Her finger violently poked out the numbers. They heard it rings. One...two...three...four...five...six... "Come on, pick up the damn phone." It continued to ring. Seven...eight...

A sleepy female voice answered. "Hello?"

"Hi, Mommy. It's me, Maggie. Um...how's your day going?" Her voice changed to sweet and childlike. Maggie rocked back and forth in place in attempts sooth herself.

"I'm so tired." They could hear her light a cigarette while she continued to talk, "Yeah. I washed the dishes this morning. Why am I so tired?" Her lungs wheezed when she

inhaled, "When are you coming home? I'm getting kinda hungry."

"What have you eaten today?" She knew the answer. It was always the same.

"I don't remember. Nothing I think? I'm so tired." She choked on the cigarette smoke, "What time is it?"

"It's a little after seven."

"When are you coming home?"

"I'll be home shortly. I got paid today. What do you want for supper? I'm buying." Pride resonated through the last statement. It was her own money and to her, it equaled power. She had earned it and no one could take it away from her. She had to hide it from her mother though. If she found it, she would drink it. All of it, every last dime.

Her mother's voice changed, "You have money?" Maggie despised that deceitful tone of voice. Sweetie-pie-greedy was the name she labeled it. "You got paid? That's great." Maggie knew what was coming next. How would she ask for the booze this time? Beg, whine or worse, by demeaning her—again. "For supper, I'd like some chicken with mashed potatoes and gravy. And some salad. Oh and Maggie, could you pick up a little something for me? From the liquor store. Just a bottle of wine." She hoped to cover up her true agenda by swiftly added, "You know, to go with the chicken. White goes with poultry, right? Please, Pumpkin."

Maggie cringed. There it was, Pumpkin. She resented her mother's addiction. Another night with Mom-the-drunk. Her chest tightened, but she was determined to not give in to her mother's alcoholism. "Mom, I'm not using my money to buy

42

you booze. I worked too hard for this money and I'm not wasting it on booze." She waited for it... and it always came. It had become routine over the last few years. Her temples started to throb with the pressure of dealing with her mother's emotional abuse.

"You little bitch! Who do you think you are? I worked my ass off at that shit hole plastics plant so you could go to that fancy pants school of yours. You owe me. You owe me big time. You rotten little bitch. All I want is one fuckin' bottle of wine." She was yelling so loud she hacked out a wheeze, "Ah, fuck you! You're not worth my fuckin' breath. You're nothing but a stupid assistant at a cheap-ass TV station. Fuck you, you little bi..."

Maggie's voice turned hard and cold. "I'll bring home dinner." Without any emotion, she gently hung up the phone. Discouraged by her mother's behavior and the effect it had on her own life, she leaned back against the wall and slid down to the booth's floor. She slowly picked up her things and crammed them into her gapping purse. With a stone-cold expression, she trudged toward the coffee shop, to a smiling Tommy.

Brogan was perplexed, "Christ. Do you know who that was?"

"No." Richard was changing a tape and not fully paying attention.

"That's Maggie Hunt."

Richard shrugged, "So? Who?"

"You know, Maggie Hunt. The newscaster, for Channel 7. Jesus Richard, don't you watch the local news? She on every night at five o'clock."

"Oh yeah, the pretty redhead. That was her?" He labeled the next tape - 'CASH #2'. Snickering he showed Brogan, "What da ya think?"

"Cute." He swung the camera back to the booth, "You never know, do you? Poor girl. I mean, what people go through in their lives and no one else knows."

Richard softly disclosed, "My Dad drank." He swallowed hard and tried not to show any emotion. "One day my Dad came home beyond drunk and started slapping my older brother around. My sister tried to help my brother out but all she got was a backhander in the head. She flew headfirst into a wall and split her forehead wide open. When my Mom walked in, my sister was leaning against the wall with a bloody hand on her forehead and my Dad swing at anything that moved. I guess my Mom decided she'd finally had enough 'cause she grabbed him by his shirt collar and threw him out the front door. I still remember her yelling at him through the locked door, "Its either me and kids, or the booze and bars. Your choice. Now get the hell out of here and sober up you ugly old bastard.'"

"Your Mom?" Brogan couldn't believe it.

"Yep. Pretty brave too, considering Mom only stood five foot nothing and Dad weighed almost two hundred and ninety pounds."

"What happened?" He hoped he wasn't prying. Richard never talked much about his childhood. Brogan chalked it up to a lot of bad memories that Richard wanted to forget about.

"Dad came home two days later. Promised my Mom he'd never drink again. And you know what, he never did. From that time on, I only saw my Dad drink three times. At my brother's and two of my sisters' weddings. One glass of wine during the meal, that's it. We were lucky. It could have gone another way. He could have broken down the thin wooden door and really hurt somebody. Or worse, he might not have come back at all. Mom didn't work and with five kids to feed, it would have been hell on all of us. Yep, we were lucky all right." They both fell silent, absorbing his dismal memory.

The daylight began to dissolve into night. In the monitor, they could see a little of the skyline, overtop the low roof of SPOONS. The sun was setting, bringing a deluge of conflicting colors. Brilliant crimsons, heavy greys, and soft lilac, mixed with a pale green the color of lime pulp. In its own timeless leisure, the daylight disintegrated, baptizing the night with darkness. In its place, streetlights flickered and danced their way fully lit. Slashes of yellow-white light streaked across the inky asphalt from the opened shops. Night was settling in and the mood of the streets began to creep into the air. When darkness took over the night—so did its people. Souls of the evening were a different species. They lived in a world that had its own set of rules. Warping each rule to fit their particular lifestyle and circumstances. These were the distorted rules that every police officer understood and waged war against.

The officers sat silent, watching as cars passed by filled with passengers. Working people ran for their trains in the dimly lit streets. They were going home to their safe worlds, while Richard and Brogan prepared for what was yet to come.

Brogan swung the camera toward SPOONS. The man had finished his pie and Tommy had cleared away his plate. He now sat quietly reading his paper and enjoyed a cigarette.

Out from the darkened alley, a young woman clumsily fumbled with her oversized tote bag. She held onto it by one handle while digging through the stack of files it contained. Her shoulder-length blonde hair kept falling in her eyes making it difficult to see inside the bag. So she tucks it behind her ears. She looked up long enough to cross the street safely. She continued to dig into the tote, her hand finally coming out with what she had been searching for, her pager. She read the message, then rolled her eyes. Shifting the tote onto her shoulder, she headed for the phone booth. Reaching into the pocket of her faded jeans, she pulled out a coin and pushed it into the slot. She methodically pressed the buttons. Listening to the musical tone the numbers made, it reminded her of a song from her high school days. She hummed while she waited for her friend to answer. The phone rang, one...two...

"Hello?"

"Okay, what so God damned important that you think you can leave a message on my office pager?" She was noticeably pissed off, "My pager read, CALL ROSIE - RUSH! So what's up?"

"It happened. it finally happened! I can't believe it finally happened!" Her words spilled out in one long stream.

"Slow down, slow down. What's happened?" She hadn't heard her friend this excited in ages.

"He asked me out to dinner. Isn't it wonderful? He finally asked me out on an official dinner date."

"Who asked you out?" She was getting annoyed by her friend's speed talking, "and for Christ sakes, slow down."

"You know. The guy from the cafe."

"What guy from the cafe?"

"The guy I've been telling you about for the last two months. Mary, you weren't paying attention again, were you? Christ Mary!"

She knew Rosie had her there. "Um...refresh my memory. Look, I talk to so many people in a day, I sometimes get things mixed up." It was a pathetic excuse but it was the best she could create on a second's notice.

"Anyway. This guy comes into the same cafe where I eat lunch every afternoon."

"Yeah." She wasn't paying attention again. She was correcting figures on some data sheets she had jammed against the side of the booth's glass wall.

The crackling sound of the pages was driving Richard nuts. He adjusted the knobs here and there until he eliminated most of the interference.

"Well, about two months ago, we started talking. Nothing heavy, just casual shit. You know, the weather, the price of gas. Crap like that."

Hearing the pause in her friend's words, she added her usual, "U-huh."

"Then last month, our conversations started to get more personal. You know...are you single? Any children? How old are you? Do you live in the city? Those kinda questions."

"Oh, yeah." She flipped the stapled page over and squinted at the fine printing.

"Okay, so about two weeks ago he started sitting at my table. Like, right at my table." Her voice jumped two octaves.

"Yeah." Mary raised her voice to mimic her enthusiasm. She flipped back the first page to double-check a number. The receiver slipped out from behind her ear, nearly falling off her shoulder. "Shit!"

"What?"

"Nothing. Keep going." She repositioned the receiver and held it at a different angle with her shoulder.

"So we've been kinda eating lunch together for about a month now." Rosie heard the sound of paper crumpling as her friend turned the page over again. That sound pissed her off. She knew her friend wasn't listening fully and tested her. "So we ate pink elephant stew and roasted bales of purple wheat."

"What?" She wasn't sure what she heard but knew it wasn't normal, "You ate what?"

"You're not listening. Fuck, you piss me off. Some friend you are? One of the most important things in my life has just happened to me and you can't even be bothered to fully pay attention. Fuck you!" Rosie slammed down her phone.

Inside the booth, Mary hung her head down and talking to herself, "Now you've done it you stupid, stupid idiot. Why didn't you ever listen?" She continued to chastise herself while she searched for another quarter. Immediately, she called her friend back.

The phone rang. One...two...three...

"Yeah." She was really angry so it came out bitter.

"Don't hang up. Please. I'm sorry. I'm an asshole." She waited for Rosie to talk but the pause was longer than usual so she added, "A big stupid asshole."

"No, you're not. You're a *giant* stupid asshole."

"I deserved that." After another long pause they both laughed, "Okay, I'll listen now. I promise. Let's see. You've been eating lunch together for a couple of weeks now and the questions were getting personal. Is that right?" She put the papers back in her black tote bag and dropped it to the floor.

Brogan dropped the camera's focus to the floor too. He only saw her shoes for a second or two but her thick-strapped black shoes evoked images of bondage in Brogan's mind. Richard cleared his throat. Was it meant for him or just the dry, oxygen-deprived air in the van?

She sounded surprised, "Yeah, it is. You were listening."

"Well maybe not as closely as I should have been. I'm here now, keep going.

"Well, like I was saying. We've kinda been eating lunch together but it's gotten closer than that."

"Closer? In what way?"

"Last week Ryan and Bernie were about to sit with us at lunch and he made this big deal about sitting beside me in the booth. Later I had my hands under the table and he reached over and took my hand into his. It was so innocent. There was no stupid sexist 'come on' lines he just held my hand. It was so sweet. He even looked me in the eyes and smiled at me. I thought my damned heart was going to jump out my blouse."

"And you didn't see this coming?"

"Shut up!" Rosie blew out a held breath. "Anyway, since then we've been holding hands and yesterday, he...he...kissed me."

"On the lips...in public? What a cad!" Mary loved teasing her bashful friend.

"No, on the cheek." She heard Mary giggling, "What?" She realized her friend was laughing at her but decided to let it go. "Anyway, right there in front of everyone else. I was so embarrassed."

Knowing her so well, Mary was pretty sure her friend was blushing on the other end of the phone. "Sounds really sweet." She envied Rosie's innocents. Hers had vanished years ago in the back seat of a Datsun. She longed for those mysterious romantic adventures of virginity. When every kiss, every touch, is a quest for some great unknown pleasure. She would never experience those first thrilling moments again. She knew how the dance of sex and romance was performed. Her own virtue was gone and she loathed that loss.

"Today he asked me out for dinner. Well, sort of." The last bit came out discouraged.

"What do you mean by 'sort of'?" She didn't like the sound of this.

"Um. He invited me to dinner at his place."

"Oh." So this was Rosie's dilemma.

"Yeah."

"Does that scare you?"

"A little." Mary patiently waited for her friend to say it all. "Okay, it scares me a lot. Christ, dinner alone at his apartment?"

"It's okay to be scared. It's a big step."

"Oh no, there's NO big step here. You know I'm saving myself for marriage." Her voice was totalitarian.

"Oh, yeah, I forgot." The next question came out of her mouth before she could stop herself. "Um, does he know about that?"

"That's the problem. I haven't told him."

"Well, it's not something that comes up in casual conversation often. Virginity is kind of a taboo subject these days. Shit, I can't believe I'm having this conversation about it right now. Even I know it's with you and it's still kinda weird."

"That's the problem. How in the hell am I gonna tell him about this?" She sounded anxious.

"Rosie, if you can't talk to him about this, what kind of relationship are the two of you gonna have in the future?" It was a harsh statement but that what friends do. They ask those hard-ass questions.

"Fuck I hate you." Rosie blew out another deep breath. "But you're right."

"Sorry."

"Don't be, you are right." The silence between the two of them hung heavy over the phone.

Mary waited a few minutes. "So, it looks like you need a game plan. Let me think here." She hummed a little, "Oh. Have you accepted his invitation?"

"Sort of, I told him I'd think about it. He went kinda weird for a second when I said that but then Ryan came and sat with us and that defused the situation."

"That's actually a good thing. Let me think. Have you given him any indications that you might want to...you know? Do it."

She screamed it, "Absolutely not!"

"Relax, already. Christ, you hurt my eardrums."

"Sorry. No, I've been very careful not to lead him on."

"And he's been pretty shy with you too, right?"

"Yeah, I guess he has." That made her feel a little better.

"Did it ever occur to you that maybe he feels the same way you do? Maybe he feels weird about bringing up the subject too? You are pretty hot...and maybe he's scared too. I mean, you two have only talked in the cafe, right?"

"Right..."

"Well, it's not something that should be discussed in a public place, right?"

"Right."

"When's this date supposed to happen?"

"Saturday night."

"Okay, this is the plan. Somehow you need to get him alone. Someplace quiet and neutral. But with other people around, in case it goes badly. I got it, The Garden Court Yard one over on Front Street. Yeah, that should do it. It's perfect."

"Perfect for what?" Rosie was not a schemer like Mary-the-Conspirator.

"That's where you're gonna make it perfectly clear to him that you have no intention of sleep with him until you're married to him."

"Holy Christ! You want me to just tell him straight out that I'm saving myself? Holy Mother of Jesus."

"Yep. Straight out."

"But what if he gets mad and doesn't want to see me anymore?"

"Then you haven't wasted too much of your precious dating time on a jerk that only wants a relationship with premarital sex."

"Fuck you're brutal."

"Yeah, I know." After a slight pause, she joked, "You can call me horrible names if it'll make you feel better."

"Nah. It's no fun when you give me permission." She took another deep breath. "And once again, you're absolutely right. Damn, I hate it when you're right. It's a good game plan though. One of your finest."

"Um, you've missed something here."

"What did I miss?"

"What if he has the same values as you do? Did you ever think of that possibility?"

"No, I didn't. Do you think he might?"

"There's only one way to find out. Talk to him. He might surprise you." She encouraged, "Rosie, don't give up hope yet."

"Hope is a four-letter word. Come to think of it, so is love."

"Stay positive. Call me either way, okay. Um ...it looks like I gotta go, somebody else is coming to use the phone. Like I said, give me a call and let me know what happens. You Okay?"

"Yeah, I'm okay." There was a slight pause, "Hey Mary, thanks."

"No problem."

"Love ya pal. Bye" She hung up her phone and the line buzzed in Mary's ear.

She hung up the phone too. She studied the papers in her tote. She shook her head to herself, "Nope. I need sustenance first. Oh ya baby, pizza." She snapped up her belongings and slipped out the door. Just outside the booth, Mary passed by a middle-aged woman and by the look on her face; she had good news to tell whoever she was about to call.

Mary smiled her way, "Good evening."

The lady dropped her head shyly and mumbled back at her, "Evening". Over her shoulder, Mary watched the lady enter the booth. She shook her head at the mysterious reaction of the lady. But being none of her business, she simply shrugged as she made her way to Tony's.

The man at SPOONS had finished reading his newspaper. After slowly rising from his table, he left the paper at another table and paid his bill. Tommy and exchanged words. Tommy laughed at something the man said as he left. It appeared as though he might be making his way to the payphone. His limp had worsened so he was taking his time.

In the booth, the lady quickly dropped her quarter and happily poked the numbers happily. One ring...two...three...

"Hello?"

"It's me."

"You're calling late. What's up?"

"I had another dream last night and this one was splendid"

"Which kind? The good kind or the bad kind?"

"Oh baby, it was the fabulous kind!" she bopped excitedly in place. "I was at the beach."

"What kinda beach?"

She rubbed her finger along the rough texture on the phone, "Let's see, I was ..." she cleared her throat and closed her eyes, setting the scene so she could express the emotions and words right. "The dream started with the image of a Bahamian beach. Soft white sand with blue-green waves rolling into the shore. Tall palm trees that bent towards the ocean, creating pockets of refreshing shade. And there was only one set of footprints running along the beach"

She whispered, "I can see it."

"So can I," Richard muttered.

His partner echoed, "Me too."

Her voice became soft and throaty, "Behind a jumble of smooth rocks was a small pool of aquamarine water glistening in the sun. A delicate breeze blew ripples across its surface. As I walked towards it, the heat of the sand branded the bottom of my feet. I needed to cool off in its calm serenity. The sun's rays beat down upon my skin as I slide into its coolness. When I settle on the pool's bottom, its wetness enveloped me up to my waist. I feel its liquid euphoria glide between my thighs, teasing at my pleasure zone, with each movement the water makes."

"Oh, that sounds so exotic. But wouldn't your bathing suit dull the sensation of the water? Clothes numb the sensations you know?"

"Bathing suit? What bathing suit?" Her voice returned to its regular tone. "Hell, I was bare-ass naked in the Bahamas. And Honey, in my dreams, I'm always five foot ten, thin as a rail, long dark hair with boobs the size and hardness of coconuts. I'm always dripping with jewelry and never worried about money or men. That's why my dreams are the best. Now hush up, I wasn't done. I'm only getting warmed up."

"Keep going, I'm all ears." She prodded her on.

"Where was I?"

"Pleasure zone - movement in the water," she prodded again.

She inhaled to bring herself back to where she had been. The soft tone returned. "Oh yeah. I splashed the cool water over my body to refresh myself from the heat of the sun. My exposed skin reacts with goosebumps. My nipples become hard and erected. I close my eyes and put my head back to relax. Within minutes the sun reheats my skin and it's smooth tanned texture returns. With my eyes being closed, I'm transformed into a blind man, hearing everything around me. I hear the sound of the waves rushing toward the shoreline, gulls squawking in the far-off blue sky, and the breeze rustling through of the fronds of a nearby palm tree. All of a sudden, I sense that I'm not alone. I open my eyes to discover a man standing over me. Without invitation, he slid into my private aqua pool and guides himself to a spot opposite me. The motion of him entering the water creates more soft waves that splash against my hot skin. The cool water makes my flesh react as before, hard erect nibbles and tiny goosebumps. The sun was high behind him, shadowing his face. I ask myself, "Who is this man? Do I know him? He seems familiar, but who is he?" I am not afraid of this stranger. He playfully pushes water toward me, creating more gentle waves that teased at me. I respond with a girlish giggle and send waves back to him.

Without a sound, he swims slowly forward stopping directly in front of me. His face is still shadowed from me. I still have no fear of this stranger. With a sultry smile, I make him understand that his intentions were welcome and desire. Bending slightly, he scooped up my foot. I let out a long sexy sigh. His strong hands massage it slowly and gently. I am in heaven. I close my eyes again to enjoy the full effects of his manual work. Each stroke and point of pressure was pure pleasure. In one seamless motion, he releases the first foot and started the same skill on my other foot. I let out a deep moan, letting him know that he was pleasing me. He cups my heel in his one hand while sliding the other up the back of my calf. I hold my breath with anticipation. How high would his hand go? Should I stop him? No, I tell myself, let it happen. His hand stops behind my knee. He releases my heel to move his other hand behind my opposite knee. He kneels squarely before my legs. I want to open up and let him rush inside but decide differently. He would have to wait, to work for it. I play coy. Innocence is

Sexy...erotic. He attempts to pull apart my knees but I resist. My virtue must be preserved. He tries again. Once more I resist. I feel his hand slip higher up my thighs and he pressed his body rigidly against my shins. I feel his excited manhood and relish the thoughts of him pushing deep into me. I could no longer resist. I had let him in. Again, he pulls apart my legs, this time, I resisted no more. I allowed him to force himself between my trembling legs. I feel his hips brush against my inner thighs, letting my knees spread wider. My needs were hotter than the sun and they too need to be quenched. The water between us rushes over my body, adding to the intense sensation. Abruptly, he lifts my legs higher, positioning me where he wanted me. Even though I still couldn't see his shadowed face, I willingly surrender to his masculine control. Peering across my extended body, my swollen breast poking through the surface of the water, exposing my harden nipples. That when he finally..." Her voice dropped to a whisper, "There's somebody outside and he's a man. I gotta go."

"But you didn't finish the dre..." the conversation ended instantly when the caller slammed down the receiver.

Gathering her sweater together, she lowered her head into its partly hiding her face just in case he had heard anything she had said. She bolted through the doors, mumbled 'evening' and trotted past the van's front, then vanished out of sight.

With a stunned expression, the man watched her scurry away. Shrugging his shoulders, he entered the booth again, putting in his quarter to make a call. One ring, two, three, four, five, six, seven rings...still no one answered. He dug out the coin and carefully returned it in his pocket. He left the booth and lit up another cigarette while studying the night sky for a moment. His limp is getting more noticeable as he made his way across the street and disappeared beyond Tony's Pizzeria, this time he headed east.

From around the corner of the southern building walked a woman with a bulky package of diapers tucked under her arm. After checking the time on her watch, she sped up her pace. In the booth, she leaned back hard, wedging the package between her and the wall. The quarter fell with a clank and the buttons ticked as she stabbed at them. She closed her eyes while she waited. After the fourth ring someone answers.

"Hello?"

"Hi, it's me."

"Wow. You're running late."

"Yeah, sorry. I got a call from our western office just as I was locking up. They're two hours behind us, ya know?" mocking her Ukrainian boss. "Anyway, they didn't receive the

Fax I send them this afternoon, so I had to re-Fax it again and that old piece of poop fax machine wouldn't work. Took me twenty minutes to get the darn thing to warm up again. I sent it four times before they got all six pages of it. Sorry, I'm so late."

"Don't worry about it. The kids are fed, bathed and in bed waiting for Mommy to tuck them in when she gets home. Johnny got his math test back and he has great news to tell you."

She undid the top button of her blouse. "A good mark?"

"No way, not telling, it's Johnny's news."

"Tease. Anyway, I'm on my way. Oh yeah, I got more diapers too."

"That's good, I only had one left."

"When she's finally potty-trained, we should take the same money we spend on diapers each week and put it in a money jar. Heck, we could go on vacation within the year."

"Wonderful idea. Boy oh boy, we could sure use a vacation in the sun. Shall we go to France, Spain or Hawaii?"

"No, I was thinking more like Florida. Disney World should please everyone." She pulled the elastic band from her ponytail and let it fall into long brunette ribbons.

Light-hearted sarcasm filled his quick comeback. "One can only dream."

"Ha, ha, very funny." She stifled a yawn. "Well, I'm going to go now. See you in fifteen minutes. Love ya."

"Love ya too. Bye."

She didn't wait for him to hang up. She was too tired for telephone etiquette. She slipped her arm behind her to catch the package diapers before it fell to the dirty floor. Hugging them tightly like an overstuffed teddy bear she headed straight past the van and ways gone.

"That sucked. She didn't thank him for all the extra work he did."

Richard didn't understand Brogan's statement, "What extra work?"

"You know, babysit kids. Feeding them, bathing them, that work."

"First of all, it's NOT work. It's being a parent. Furthermore, Father's don't babysit their children, they parent them." Richard was almost yelling it at him.

"Okay Dad, I got it. Jesus, relax already." More tension he didn't mean to create.

"Besides, maybe she doesn't have to. Did it ever occur to you that he might be a stay home Dad?"

Surprise washed across his face. "Never thought of that."

"My next-door neighbor Dave does it."

"Your neighbour Dave? Big Dave Hogan?"

"Yep. Last October he got laid off at the factory and his wife got hired full time at the hospital two weeks later. She goes to work and he raises the three kids. He says he loves it and she's happy too. Seems to work out just fine for them."

"We've got another one." Brogan pointed with his chin, "On the right."

Richard was relieved that someone showed up right then. The mood in the van was excruciatingly tense.

Brogan swung the camera to the next suspect. "Relax. It's just a kid."

"Oh yeah right, kids never do anything wrong." Sarcasm, a cop's favorite tool, "Kids sell drugs too. Or did you forget?"

"Yeah, yeah whatever." He was getting fed up with Richard's preachiness and the tension it brought, "He looks about fourteen, fifteen tops. Dresses nice, probably has rich parents." Richard shook his head. Leave it to Brogan to notice the designer clothing. Brogan focussed the camera in closer and Richard adjusted the recording volume.

He stood outside the booth, kicking at the ground like a five-year-old. He was trying to talk himself into something. Nearly out of range, the microphone could barely pick up his voice, so Richard cranked up the volume to its max.

"I can do it. Yep, I can do this." He began to pace in a small circle, round and round, "Come on, this ain't that hard. Getting my nipple pierced, now that was hard. Remember the pain. Now that was agony. I can do this." He was looking down at his feet as he paced and when he stopped to look at the booth, he felt slightly dizzy. "I can do this. Yep, I can do this. Yep." He let out a low grunt, "Nope! I can't do this. Shit! I can't do this." Angry with himself, he stomped his feet and hit his sides with his arms. "What is wrong with me? Christ, I've done this at least a dozen times before." The self-pep talk was getting louder and louder, "I can do this! I can do this! Shit, shit, shit! No, I can't." He kicked the booth and discovered

another kind of pain that made him hop on one foot and howl, "Damn it. Damn it. Damn it!"

Two women who were watching him from across the street sped up their pace. To them, he looked like a drugged up teenager that was about to freak out.

"Oh Christ, just do it. Just do it. What's the worst that can happen? It's a 50/50 chance. Right? Just do it. Now. Right now!" He threw open the booth doors and stood squarely in front of the phone. Inhaling a deep breath, he dug out a quarter and pushed it into the slot. The dial tone buzzed in his ear for along while. "Do it!" he murmured. He had memorized the number but his hand was trembling so hard he ended up pushing a three instead of a two, "Shit!" He slammed down the receiver. Taking another deep breath, he fished out the quarter from the phone's coin cup. "Again, now!" he ordered himself. In went the quarter and he firmly punch the numbers again.

The phone began to ring. One ring...two...three...

"Hello?" It was a young girl's voice.

Panic hit him and he slammed down the receiver. "Shit, she answered. Shit." His breathing came in gasps. Leaving the booth and he paced some more. This time the pep talk turned harsh. "Really bright jack ass. Hang up the phone. Brilliant." He chastised himself over and over as he paced.

Inside the van, the two cops were killing themselves laughing. He was a teenage boy making that horrible first call to a girl he was clearly enamored with.

63

"Christ, I remember that gut-twisting feeling. Polly Cedar. She was so damn sexy and I wanted to take her to the movies in the worst way. Took me seven calls over three days, but I finally did it."

"You mean to tell me that 'Richie the sweet talker' couldn't do it on the first try either?"

"Nope. Polly scared the beJesus out of me. She did most of the talking, as it turned out she liked me too. Thank fuckin' God too, the way I was babbling, I would've never gotten a date with her."

"Wait. He's back." Brogan focussed on the boy's shaking hand, then pulled back to a full picture of him in the booth. With that, the tension in the van relaxed.

He put another quarter into the slot and punched the numbers again. The phone began to ring again. One ring...two...three...

"Hello?" It was the same girl's voice, "Hello?"

Instant paralyzes. His mouth simply wouldn't work. He tried to speak but nothing would come out. His thoughts were so jumbled when he did talk, it came out as gibberish. "You...I like...um ..." anxiety made him hang up again. With his head hanging down, his frustrations took over. "I'm such a stupid idiot. Shit!" He straightened up tall and punched the booth's doors. The door swung back, hitting him square in the head. That was the moment he decided he wasn't built for violent macho behavior. Leaving the booth, he paced back and forth in front of it, "Last try, I can do this. I gotta do this. Shit!" He stopped to face the doors. "Last try." He stepped inside, plunked the next quarter into its opening. Determined, he dialled her again...one ring...two...

"Hello?" It was the same girl but her voice wasn't as sweet as before. "Who is this? Listen here, you pervert, I'm calling the cops on you. So you better stop callin' here." Her voice was an odd mixture of anger and fear, "My Dad's in the other room and he can beat you up, so stay away from me. He's big and he can ..."

He broke in, "Cindy, it's me, Tim."

She stayed silent for a few moments, not sure who Tim was. "Tim who?"

"Yeah, Tim from third-period history class. I sit in the back row by the window."

"Back row? Oh yeah, Timmy Holtz, right?" Her voice turned gentle and pleasant again. "Hey, did you just call here? Like a couple of times in a row?"

"Um, yeah, sorry about that. I...um...I got...um ..." Now, what was he going to say? 'I got so nervous I turned into a big babbling butt head.'

Sensing his embarrassment, she cut in, "So, why'd you call me anyway?"

He almost hung up again but sucked in a deep breath to settle his nerves. "I was calling to ask you to ...um, if you'd...um..." He took another breath, "Would you like to come to a party at my house on Saturday night?" His heart pound so hard he thought it might explode. Mentally he chanted, 'Say yes, say yes, say yes, say yes'. There was a long silent pause. She wasn't saying anything. His confidence disintegrated, "I mean if you're not busy or anything?" He swallowed hard, swallowing down his disappointment. "If you don't want to come it's okay!"

She giggled, "Um...is your older brother Frankie going to be there too?"

'Yeah, I think so."

"Then I'd love to come," she squeaked and giggled nervously.

He blew out the breath he wasn't aware he was holding. Completely surprised by her acceptance of his invitation, he blurted out the first thing that popped in his head, "You would? Are you sure?"

"Yep, I'm sure. Um...but a can I bring my friend Carla?"

He detested Carla. She was an overweight, pizza faced, motor mouth whose greatest joy in life was bad-mouthing other people and spreading gossip. Unfortunately, he knew that if Carla didn't come, Cindy wouldn't come either. They went everywhere and did everything together. He had no choice. "Yeah. I guess it would be okay."

"Great. I'll talk to you about it tomorrow, in history class, okay?" she giggled again.

"Okay, great. See ya there." He hung up the phone before she got a chance to say good-bye. He stood staring at the phone that dangled in front of him. He quietly muttered to himself, "She said yes," His hands were still trembling. "Oh Christ, she said yes. She's actually coming to *my* party." Now he was really nervous and swallowed hard to ease the lump in his throat. Immediately, he hushed out of the booth; spun in spot and yelled, "She said yes! She said YES!" He jumped three feet in the air, then punched a hole in the night sky. Tim whooped and leaped his way out of the camera's view.

Across the street at the coffee shop, Tommy was holding open the door for Maggie. Tommy waved goodnight as he watched the way her ass disappear down the street.

"What a fuckin' stupid moron. He didn't catch it, did he?" Brogan was livid. "Bitch."

"Nope." Richard was furious too. Not at the girl but at the boy.

"I hate it when chicks do that. The old-is-the-guy-a-really-like-going-to-be-there-so-I-can-break-your-fucking-heart-at-the-same-time bullshit," He slapped the arm of the chair in anger.

"You know what? He's the fuckin' idiot here. It's obvious as hell that she's interested in the older brother and not him. So why didn't he notice it?"

Brogan cut in, "'cause she a conniving little bitch, that's why."

"No, it's because he's in love. Or he thinks he is. You know the old saying, 'Love is blind'...well apparently it's deaf too. She said it straight out and dumb fuck missed it. Pay attention or you lose. That's one of those life rules." Richard had that 'sermonizing father' tone to his voice and Brogan knew he wasn't going to win this argument.

Tension again.

"I still feel sorry for the moron. She's gonna crush him."

"Sounds to me like you've been there yourself. Wanna SHARE?" Richard mocked the word share. It was in this week's memo. According to the Police Department's psychiatrist, partners need to share their emotions more often and preferably while they are still on the job. "No, I don't wanna share."

Brogan shot him a lethal look, "Fuck you too."

"Such hostility?" he snorted. Then he used one of the oldest Psychological tricks known to mankind. Silence makes people talk. There is this odd human need to fill the silence. Richard sat quiet and waited. He knew what would happen next. The result was predictable. And as always, it worked.

Brogan filled the silence. "It was a long time ago, okay. And she ..."

Richard only pointed at him and roared with laughter, "Gotcha!"

"Fuck you asshole," Brogan whipped his pen at him, "Dick Head!"

That made Richard laugh even harder. So hard he almost flipped over on his already backward tilting chair.

"We got company." Brogan pivoted the camera in the other direction, "She's a looker too." As usual, he scanned her body from head to toe while she stood beside the booth.

"Knock it of pervert. I know this one. She's a good kid. She lives right around the corner from me. I think her name is Pam. My wife knows her really well. They go to the community centre together sometimes."

"Pam? No way. She looks more like a Loretta to me," Brogan had a knack for placing a name to a face that truly suited them. "No, wait, maybe...Betty Sue. One things for sure, she's a country girl. Look at those boots." Aged dark brown leather with thick belt straps that held the big silver buckles in place. Soft aged leather. The imaginary perfume of warm leather aroused Brogan's cerebral senses.

"Nope, it's definitely Pam. But you're right about the country girl thing. She's got the cutest twang when she talks." His facial expression changed from a pleasant smile to a deep scowl of disapproval. "Now, what's her husband's name? Mike, Mark...Mitch, that's it, Mitch."

"What's with the sourpuss?"

Well, I only meet him twice, once at the grocery store and once when I was pumping gas." Richard mindlessly scribbled in his note pad as he talked. "There's something about that guy that rubs me the wrong way. You know that gut feeling you get, when something looks like one thing, yet you know damn well it's something else and you can't isolate it. That's the impression I get from them two."

"What happened to make you suspected something's wrong?" Brogan had been a witness to Richard's keen sense of the concealed many times over the years.

"It was last week. When I went in to pay for my gas, the clerk was super nervous and extremely quiet. I've never known her to be the skittish kind. In fact, she's usually perky to the point of nausea. Come to think of it, he sure jerked his head around when I walked in. He paid cash and left pronto. Fast enough to make me ask Chrissie if there had been a problem. All she said was 'no more than usually' and then she changed the subject really quick. We talked about Sally's new job promotion and I left it at that. But the whole situation is still stuck in my head. My cop gut says don't trust this dude. He's trouble."

"She's in," Brogan accidentally zoomed in a little closer than he intended to. "She's been crying. Fuck man, look at her cheek." Focussing in tighter, he squirmed uneasily in his chair. He knew what he was looking at. He'd seen it too many times before.

"I knew it! That fuckin' prick! Fuck, she such a nice girl too. That's one nasty bruise. Search for others." He ordered with his fingers, "Get it on tape. Fuckin' bastard. Too bad we can't shoot bastards like him. I'd get him in one shot. Right between the fuckin' eyes. Bang." Richard blew out one long angry breath. "Sally's going to be outraged. She talks about Pam a lot. Sally never mentioned any bruises or odd behavior though, and she noticed things like that. Only talked about Pam being so sweet to everyone, young and old alike."

"Shh! Here we go." Brogan continued to search for other evidence. A bulging bottom lip and a small cut above her left eye. He recorded the bruises on her arms where strong hands had left forceful finger marks behind. The image of a dead female beating victim flashed through his memory. The one from his past he had let slip through the cracks of a male-oriented police force. It prompted him to look in those places where those types of indignities might be found on her. He fixed the camera on her neck, no marks. He was both sickened and angry at the same time. A man, one of own kind, had done this to someone weak and undeserving. "Disgusting coward," Was all he could say. Brogan forced himself to concentrate on what he was doing. In the future, she cou d use these tapes to save her life...if she wanted them to. Tragically, not all beating victims wanted to be saved.

Pam pushed the zero button.

"Jamestown Telephone, how may I help you?" The operator's voice was hard to hear over the static.

"I wanna make a collect call ta my Mama, Mrs. Marsha Larkin at ..." a late-night delivery truck rumbled by as she gave the operator the numbers.

By the time the truck had completely passed, the phone was ringing.

"Hello?"

"Good evening Ma'am. We have a collect call from a Pam Houston. Will you accept the charges?"

"Yes. That'll be fine. Thank ya kindly." A cheerful bubbly voice answered, "Howdy Honey."

"Hi ya, Mama." Pam's voice was straining to be happy. The operator disconnected and the static on the line died.

"Ya'll haven't called in a while. What's new?" Marsha knew Pam only called her Mama when she was in trouble and needed someone to rescue her. Marsha wondered what happened this time.

"Oh, I've been awful busy. You know, with my volunteerin', the house chores, and ...with Mitch." Her mood turned sullen, "It's a lot of work."

There was silence for a lengthy time, "Pam, is you all right? He's started up again, ain't he? You can tell me," Marsha's motherly tone was meant to tug at her daughter's heartstrings, "I'm here for you, no matter what. No questions asked. Just talk to me...please talk to me."

Pam stifled her tears by swallowing hard, "I know that Mama, that's why I'm a callin'. Um...I do need help." She let it all go. She stood in place and openly sobbed into the phone. Marsha held her emotions in and waited for her daughter to get herself together. Collecting her strength Pam finally asked, "Mama, I need ta come on home. I gotta leave here right now and I need money for a ticket. Mama, please help me?" She sobbed again. On the phone, she could hear her mother telling her father to immediately wire the money to her nearest West Union office.

"Oh, Mama everythin's gone haywire." She blew her nose. "I'm ascared. Send it right quick. Please, Mama, please."

The begging wrenched at Marsha's heart. "Oh Honey, Daddy's on his way to Price's General Store right now. They gots a West Union office in there now." Marsha took a deep breath before she asked the next question. Part of her didn't want to know the answer. "How badly are you hurt? Do you want us to come get you? We can, you know? We can be there in less than four hours."

"NO! NO! Don't come here!" Realizing she was screaming, "Oh shit, I'm sorry Mama, I'm not like myself right now. Ya'll forgive me, okay? Mama, please just send the money. I don't want ya to get mixed up in this. I don't want ya to get hurt too. I'm goin' back to the apartment to pack my bags, then I'm headin' on down to the West Union."

Marsha's words of warning came fast. "Don't go back there! He'll hurt you some more. Stay away, go to a church or better yet, to a police station. Just don't go back in there. He'll kill you." Her heart thundered through her ears, "It's just stuff. We'll send somebody to get your stuff after you're safe here back with us and away from him. Hell, we'll get you new stuff. It doesn't matter. Just don't go back there."

"Mama, it's all right. He goes to his Uncle after we have a fight. Sometimes he stays overnight," her confidence was returning. "I'll tell you what, if I think he's in there, I won't go in." It sounded like she was trying to convince her herself more than her mother.

"Fine. But you promise me that if he's in there, you'll get your arse outta there right away and go to a safe place. Promise me." She waited for a response that didn't come quick enough for her liking. She hysterically demanded, "PROMISE ME, DAMN IT!" Marsha was finally losing it, "PROMISE ME! PROMISE ME, NOW!"

"Mama, calm down. Shh. Calm down. It'll be fine. I promise you that I'll leave straight away. I promise. Now calm down. Christ Mama, ya watch your blood pressure. Y'all bring on a heart attack."

"You're right, I'll calm down." She took three deep breaths and blew them out slowly. "Okay, I'm better. Now go on get your stuff and get the hell out of there. When you get to the West Union office call us, ya hear?"

"I promise. I'm comin' home by train. So I won't be gettin' home until mornin'. Can you come get me at the station?"

"Of course we will. You just call us when you get there. No matter what time it is. Besides, I ain't sleepin' a hoot until I know my baby girl is safe and away from that lunatic. You hurry on up Honey, before he comes back. Be careful. And Honey, remember it's just stuff. We can always get you more stuff. Now get yourself goin'." She was chocking up. She wasn't sure what was going to happen later that night and there might not be another chance to say it, "And Pamela...I love you, Honey Girl."

"I love you too, Mama," Pam swallowed hard, "I gotta go. I'll see you tomorrow...you'll see. Bye Mama." She pressed down the receiver with her finger. The dial tone went dead. In the silence, Pam's shoulders shook hard with each deep sob.

Richard turned down the volume. He couldn't listen to her cry. He turned his chair toward the radio, "I'll call for somebody to follow her. I'll be damn if that rotten fucker's gonna get away with this. If she can get away, she'll be all right."

"Sounds right." An evil grin formed on Brogan's lips "What do you say I pay the asshole a friendly little visit next week? I'm on nightshift with Sheridan and he likes visiting cowardly pricks too."

"I'd appreciate that." With a sharp nodded Richard agreed to his offer.

"I thought you would." While Richard gave the night Captain the particulars, Brogan followed her with the camera. As she passed the pizza place, he noticed an old man was standing in the shadows of a doorway. Brogan focussed the camera on the man with the long reddish ponytail, "Hey, look at the old hippie over by the pizza place!"

"Yeah man, nice beads and bandana man." Richard played up the sixties lingo. "Christ, he's gotta be in his sixties." Richard was happy for the distraction. Like brogan, he too had seen the end result of women trying to leave their abusive partners. Most brutal—several fatal.

"That's would be about right. If he was 20 years old in the early '60s, he'd be around 60, 62 by now. Wow, time flies."

"Were where you in 1967?" That particular year was Richard's favorite.

"Let's see, I would've been 12 years old. Oh yeah, grade 7, Mrs. Morton's class. She had these huge boobs. Christ, I used to watch those plump mounds jiggle for hours. White cotton blouses still turn me on. How about you?" Although the camera was focused on the Hippie, brogan kept an eye on the street for Pam.

"Nope, white cotton shirts only remind me of the Nuns at my school. That and wooden yardsticks." Richard's body shivered hard, "Yardsticks still scare the shit out of me."

"No, you putz. How old were you in '67?"

"I was 14. That was the summer I met Sally. I'm surprised she ever talked to me again after the first day we met." Richard felt the need to focus on the happier times between Sally and him. "What an asshole I was. My best buddies bet me five bucks I couldn't get a date with the pretty blonde by the jute box. You see she was sixteen, an older woman. But hey, five bucks is five bucks, right? So with that in mind, I aimed to impress her right away." Richard laughed at himself, "I slicked down my sideburns, put on my best Shawn Cassidy smile and went for it. I was trying to play it super-cool but it came across more like dumb-fuckin'-asshole. Anyway, I strutted over to her table and made that cool gaze down my nose like James Dean. I even paused for effect. Yeah, it had a great effect all right. I lost my balance, fell face forward into her table and spilled orange soda all over her pale blue sundress. Christ, was she ever pissed off. She started screaming and throwing food at me. Yep, I fell in love with her right then and there. But before I could get her name, she stormed off madder than hell. It took me another two weeks to pry her phone number out of her friends. They weren't sure if they should give it to me, considering how much she detested me. Took me another five weeks of dogging her before she agreed to go out on a date with me."

"Wait, what's 'dogging'? I've never heard that expression before."

"Um... following her. Showing up in the same places she does, asking lots of questions about her. I even took photos. It took me eleven days to figure out her schedule."

Brogan roared, "Fuck Richard...you were stalking her."

"Shit! I guess I was." He never realized he had been doing it. He was in love with her and really meant her no harm. He would have to look at stalkers a little differently now.

"Who's the sick pervert now?" Brogan grabbed the chance to get back at Richard.

Richard ignored him. "Sally gave me such a hard time on our first date. I damn near left halfway through it. Problem was, my buddies were watching and I still wanted that five bucks. So I stuck it out and did my penance. By the time I walked her home, she had warmed up to me enough to let me kiss her goodnight." Richard cracked up, "My asshole buddies catcalled us from the hedges embarrassing both of us. Stupid jerks' didn't know I really had a thing for Sally. She got completely flustered and ran into her house. I yelled at those dick heads all the way down to the wharf. And as I recall *after* I got my five bucks, I threw one of the fuckin' assholes right in the bay. Anyway, the next day I went to Sally's to ask her out again. And to my surprise, she said yes. We've been together ever since." The smile on Richard's face said it all. Pure domestic bliss.

Brogan had been watching the old guy in the camera the whole time. "What in the fuck is that hippie up to? He's just standing there gawking into the pizza place. He hasn't moved more than ten feet in the last ten minutes."

"He's probably stoned out of his skull, got the munchies and can't figure out how to get through the door." They were both getting tired and giddy, "Yeah, he's visually impaired and needs a seeing-eye munchies dog." They both cracked up. They couldn't help it, the hippie was such a bazaar sight, an old sixties geezer totally zombie-ing out at the pizza joint.

Wiping away tears, Brogan finally got himself under control, "No, I think he's watching for something or maybe somebody."

FOUR

At that moment a bunch of boys barrelled passed the front of the van, whooping and shouting at the top of their lungs.

"You're it, Teddy!"

He flipped him the finger, "No you're it, shit head." His accent was heavy enough to know he wasn't from this part of the city.

When they reached the booth the fighting really started.

The smaller boy with the short rusty colored hair and freckles commanded, "I'm first, you fuck wads."

The tall thin guy yelled louder, "Like fuck you are, shit head."

"You're both dick heads. It's my fuckin' money, so I'm going first. Don't like it, go suck shit." With his thick muscular body, he plowed right between the two of them and grabbed the phone. The space in the booth was so tight that someone ended up sticking their butt out the doors. Angus laughed like crazy as he poked his butt in and out of the booth. Harry plopped the coin into the slot and punched the numbers. The phone only rang once.

An answering machine kicked in, it was a sexy woman's voice, "Hi, you've reached Dotty The Hottie. I'm not here. You know what to do. So..." After a strange extended pause came the usual 'Peeeeeeep' sound.

He lowered the tone of his voice to sound more radio sounding, "Oh folk's, that's too bad she's not home." The other boys groaned in the background to mock the radio crew's disappointment. "Dottie, this is Mat Martin from RocTalk FM and you were our caller of the night. Tonight's prize for the Twilight Travel Trivia was an all-expenses-paid trip for two to Cuba. But you weren't home, so you couldn't answer tonight's trivia question. Sorry, darling, you didn't win. You try to have yourself a nice evening. Bye-bye." He slammed down the phone and all three roared. Harry managed to mutter, "Wait 'til 'Dotty The fuckin' Hottie' gets a load that message. It'll piss her off for days."

"Oh great, crank calls. Just what I wanted to listen to." Richard wasn't fond of teenage boys. He had raised two girls and in Richard's mind, teenage boys were nothing but trouble, whether it was at girls or the world at large.

"Smartass, brats. They know damn well the call display will read 'payphone'. Little Scottish bastards."

"Irish," Brogan corrected.

"Whatever," he snapped back, "Still little bastards."

"It's your turn, Angus," Harry shoved the quarter at him, "You make the most awesome calls."

Angus poked at the numbers. On the third ring, someone picked up.

"Hello?" A sleepy girl answered, "Hello?"

He yelled into the mouthpiece, "Stop fuckin' calling me!" and hung up.

Dumbfounded, Teddy jabbed Angus in the arm and spun him around, "What in the hell was that all about?"

"Relax, you'll see later, I'm not done yet." Angus had a plan. He always had a plan. "Besides it's your turn freckle face."

"I'm not real good at this shit guys. You know that?" Teddy didn't like doing this sort of stuff. It felt wrong but he would do it so Angus and Harry would keep him around. "It's a waste of a quarter. You go ahead again Harry, you're better at it than me."

"You got that right, dip shit! Okay. Who to piss off now?" The boys shuffled around in the crowded booth. It was Teddy's turn to stick his butt out the door. "I got it. Weirdo Wilson."

"Principal Wilson? Holy fuck!" Teddy didn't like this idea. If Wilson figured out it was them, they might get caught. Then his Mom would find out that he was still hanging around with Angus and Harry. She had told him not to play with them because they were nothing but delinquents. "No way dude. Pick somebody else."

It was too late. Harry had already put in the money and was stabbing at the numbers.

"You have reached the Wilson residence. Sorry, but we're not available at this time. Please leave a message and we will return your call as soon as possible. Thank you." Peep.

Harry changed his voice to a Middle Eastern accent, "Hello. This is Abdul from 'We Move Your Things'. I am calling you to tell you that we will be at your home at seven o'clock in the morning to pick up your furniture. I am thanking you very much." Harry hit the receiver. Angus and Harry laughed like hell but Teddy didn't even crack a smile.

Harry stopped cold and stared at him, "What's the matter with you?"

Angus' laughter died too, "Yeah, what gives?"

"Uh...I'm not feeling good. I think I ate too many fries. My guts are kinda rough." He knew he had to hide his feelings. "I think I'm gonna puke." Teddy made a sickly face, grunted a vomiting sound and hurled his head toward their feet. Harry jerked his feet out of the way and danced in spot to miss the vomit. Teddy whipped his head up and pointed at him. "Gotcha, ass wipe!" Harry slugged him in the arm.

"Give me another quarter." Harry flipped it to him. "Part two." Angus punched in the same phone number as before.

Harry looked at Teddy, "What's he doing now?"

Teddy shrugged his shoulders. "Damn if I know?"

"It's ringing." Angus' face was a picture of wickedness.

"Hello?" It was the same timid female voice as before, "Hello? Who is this?"

He yelled, "Stop fuckin' calling me!" and hung up the phone again.

"Hey, I recognize that voice, that's Becky," Teddy smiled a depraved smile himself, "She fuckin' hot."

"Becky? You mean the one with long curly hair from homeroom?"

"Yep." Angus grinned widely.

"Never mind her hair, I'm thinking about that body of hers. She's got the best rack in the whole school. When she wears that black T-shirt, the one that scoops really low, I can't think of anything else but those big round tits." Harry squeezed the air with his hands. "One of these days I'm just gonna grab a handful of those beauties. It'd be worth all the shit I'd get into." His face had a far-off dreamy look.

Angus' eyes narrowed at Harry. He couldn't stand the thought of anyone thinking about his girl that way. Angus worshipped Becky Wright, but only from a distance. He knew she would never go out with him though. They were from completely opposite worlds. She was a high-class debutante and he lived in the seedier part of town. She wore the latest designer clothes and his wardrobe came from the local thrift stores. That didn't stop him from thinking of Becky as his girl though. He didn't like that horny look in Harry's eyes, "In your fuckin' dreams asshole. She's way too good for you."

Teddy noticed the mean look forming on Angus' face and quickly changed the subject. "Who's next?" He jabbed his finger into Harry's rib cage, "Come on big shot, your turn."

"No, it's your turn." Both Angus and Harry said it at the exact same time. Now he would have to make a call. His stomach twisted into a tight aching knot. He hated doing this kind of thing. It was so...childish. And besides, what if they got caught? "But...but I don't know any trick phone calls."

"What a wuss!" Harry poked him back, "Wimpy, wimpy, wimpy!"

"You're not scared, are ya?" Making clucking noises, Angus taunted him, "Buck, buck, buck. Here chicken, chicken, chicken."

Being teased in that manner infuriated Teddy to the core. Anger filled him. He would prove to them he was no chicken. "Fuck you, ya dick wads!" He pushed Angus to the outside of the booth. "Give me a fuckin' quarter?" He didn't want to do it but nobody called him a wimpy chicken. Angus flipped the coin at him, Teddy caught it in mid-air and popped it into the slot, all in one smooth motion. Closing his eyes, he started randomly punching numbers. He counted out loud until he had pushed all seven numbers. "One, two, three, four, five, six, seven." As it rang, his stomach wrenched. On the third ring, someone picked up.

"Father Thomas here. How can I help you?"

Teddy froze in place. The guys knew he was in trouble when his eyes grew the size of silver dollars.

"Hello? Hello? Do you need help? Are you in trouble? Are you still there?"

He pulled the phone away from his ear and stared at the mouthpiece, "Jesus Christ! It's Father Thomas. I'm sooo fucked." He slammed the phone down, "Oh shit, Oh shit. That was my Mom's priest. I'm sooo fucked! Shit!" Right in place, he did a hysterically funny little jog while flapping his hands by his chest. To his friends, he looked kind of girly.

The other two boys burst out laughing. Angus was laughing so hard he fell backward through the booth doors and landed flat on his ass. Harry wiped his eyes after he helped him back on his feet.

Teddy paced back and forth outside the booth. "It's not funny! I'm so fucked!"

Harry grabbed him by the arm and turned Teddy around to face him. "Look. Relax already. How in the hell is he going to know it was you? Are you the only teenage boy who goes to that whacko church of yours? No. So shut up. Besides if he asks anything about tonight, just deny it 'cause right now, you're home in bed, aren't you?"

"Oh yeah, that's right." He smiled with relief, "I'm tucked in my little bed, all fast asleep like a good little boy." Lately, he had snuck out his bedroom window so many times, he had forgotten where he was actually supposed to be.

Harry let his arm go. "Did you really punch those numbers randomly?"

"Yeah, I had my eyes closed the whole time. You watched me."

"Holy shit, the weirdest things happen to you. It's like you're jinxed or something." With a Vincent Price type voice, he curled his fingers and arched over Teddy's head. "Muh ha ha. Maybe it's the curse of the Irish Idiots who've come to haunt your life forever."

"Give me another quarter?" That wicked gleam returned to eyes, Angus headed for the phone. "Phase three." Impatient, he stuck out his hand, "Come on with the quarter already."

84

Harry dug deep into his pocket. "Make it good, that's my last quarter."

"Let's see if Becky's still awake?"

Harry groaned, "Christ."

The color returned to Teddy's face, "Again?"

Angus punched in the same number while the other two boys jostled for position. Once again it was Teddy's butt hanging out the door.

"It's ringing." Two...three...

"WHO IS THIS?" A man's voice blared from the phone, "YOU LITTLE BASTARD. IF I CATCH YOU, YOU'RE DEAD MEAT. YOU HEAR ME! I'M CALLING THE TELEPHONE COMPANY RIGHT NOW TO GET A COPY OF THE TAPE FROM THE CAMERA IN THAT BOOTH..."

Angus' eyes scanned the booth for some kind of camera device. He pointed to the camera lens. "There!" He instantly dropped the phone and bellowed, "RUN!" He bolted between two boys nearly knocking Teddy on his ass. He turned around long enough to yell over his shoulder, "Come on. Let's get the fuck out of here!" Teddy eyed the dangling phone. Harry spotted the surveillance camera in the upper corner. At the exacted same time they both scrambled out after him, yelling and whooping all the way. Even with the fear of being apprehended they still didn't take the situation seriously. Angus was leaning against the pizza place trying to catch his breath when they ran past him. Harry smacked him on top of the head. Angus chased them down the street restarting the original game of tag. Teddy dodged Angus' swipe and slammed into the old hippie. He bowed his head in apology.

The old hippie only smiled and shrugged his shoulders. From behind, Angus yanked on Teddy's arm, pulling him down the right side of the alley. Coming out of the same alley came a short hairy man carrying a green duffle bag. He nodded at the old hippie before going into the pizza place.

The old hippie finally moved. He walked slowly toward the booth, curiously looking all around the streets. He pushed the doors open with his forearm and slipped his backpack onto the floor. He reached into the pocket of his tie-dyed T-shirt and fished out a quarter. His fingers fumbled with it. It took him several tries before he could get it in the slot. He pushed each button slowly and deliberately with the knuckle of his crooked index finger.

"Wow, is he ever stoned? He can't even work the fuckin' phone."

Appalled by the sight of the old hippie, Brogan muttered, "Yeah. That's how I want to retire. Stoned beyond comprehension." He tossed his pen down angrily, "What a waste?"

From the booth Copper could see inside the pizza place. He watched Tony pick up the phone.

"Tony's Pizza. What'a I get ya?" Leaning on the counter with his elbows he nestled the phone between his ear and his shoulder.

"Yeah. Hey man, I'd...um...I'd like to order a pizza."

Mindlessly, Tony reached for the order pad, "Okay...what'a size and what da ya want on it?"

"I wanna order the one with the special toppings."

That caught Tony's attention. Copper watched him stand up straight in the pizzeria window. "What'a special toppings are you'a talking about?"

Richard sat up tall in his chair and glanced at Brogan. "Special topping?"

"It's the happy herb." Richard shrugged his shoulders. "Christ Richard, their talking about pot. Now shut up and listen." The tension returned.

"Leon said it was high quality...toppings." Copper explained that he had met Leon through a friend two nights before and things were roughly explained over a quick beer at the bar.

"Youa know Leon?" Tony had to be careful.

"Yeah man, he said to come by while he was working to order the po...um ...pizza." he caught his mistake and corrected the near slip of word immediately. "Is he working?" Copper could see Leon from the booth but thought he should ask anyway.

"Well that'sa different story."

"Right on! So um...can you take my order?"

"You'a cop?" Tony asked everybody that same question.

"No way, man. Fuck the pigs." Copper's mood turned testy "Look man, all I want is some wee...pizza. Screw the bullshit. Now how much are you selling the pizza for? Leon never mentioned prices."

"All right, all right, calm'a down. What'a size you lookin' for. A small is $50.00 and a medium, she's a $125.00."

"So, how much for a large pizza?"

"A large is big'a money. 250 dollars. Cash."

"Not bad, how much for an extra-large?"

"$500.00. But that'sa lot of pizza." His Italian accent slurred the inquiring words together. "You need that much pizza?"

"Ya man, I really enjoy my pizza. I smo...eat pizza, every day. I use it for my..."

Tony cut him off, "Hey. That'sa your'a business, nota mine. I no wanna know about what you do. So, what size you'a want? You'a want large or extra large?"

"Make it an extra-large. Sounds like a large won't be enough to get us through the week."

"Okay, youa pick it up anytime youa like. Ah cash only, uh. Last'a night some asshole, he tries to pay by cheque. Whata fuckin' retard. How will I know who youa are?"

"They call me Copper" was all he said before he slowly hung up the phone and rubbed his hands together. He stared at his hands as he opened and closed them over and over again. Copper slipped his closed hand through the loop of his backpack and headed toward Tony's.

Brogan followed him with the camera. "Shit! We can't do a damn thing about this tonight. It'll blow our cover and the whole investigation."

"Shit is right. I'll have to write up a separate report on this and give it the Captain."

"Relax. Chances are we'll get him on tape selling more of his special pizzas tonight." Brogan had no tolerance for drug dealers. "God damn. We'll get the buyers on tape too. Court cases always go so much smoother with video evidence. Birdy will love us for this. Pot pusher served up on a silver platter."

Brogan focussed the camera toward the pizzeria. Copper walked across its site line. The camera caught the strain on his face as he pulled open the door.

"Fuck, look at him, he's so wrecked he can't even open the damned door. That's so pathetic." Richard agreed with him. "Yep. Drugs ruin a life."

They watched as Copper shuffled to the counter. Tony grinned as he waved his red ponytail at him. They talked briefly before Tony disappeared into the back room. From his backpack, Copper pulled a large manila envelope and dumped five bundles of twenty-dollar bills on the counter. Each bundle had a blue elastic around it. Tony rushed to the counter and swept the bundles onto the floor with the s de of the pizza box. Copper backed away when Tony yelled at him. His face angry and his arm flying in the air, he jammed the pizza box at Copper and pointed to the door. Copper bowed a thank you and sluggishly slipped on his backpack. Carefully balancing the box between his hands, he backed through the door and left the pizzeria. Tony picked the bundles off the floor and put them under the counter's half shelf. He carefully pulled off the blue elastic of one of the bundles and counted the bills under the counter.

The camera caught it all.

Slowly Copper walked back to the payphone. He leaned the pizza box on its side against the booth wall. He went through the same routine as last time, but this time a lady answered.

"Hello?" Her voice was older like his.

"It's me." His tone turned excited, "I got it!"

"Thank the Good Lord Above! When can you get here with it?"

"I'll take a cab. That way I can be there right away."

"Copper, I want to thank you. I know you need the stuff too, but thank you. God bless you for your kindness."

"It's all right. How's your hip holding up?"

"Hurt's like hell, but it'll be all right soon. Once I get this medicine in me, I'll be just fine. I've never let my arthritis stop me before and I'll be damned if it's gonna stop me now. You sound kinda edgy. Your hands hurting too?"

"Yep. Listen, I'm gonna get going. I'm kinda getting tired. The pain wears me down fast these days. I should be there in about fifteen minutes or so."

"Okay. God's speed Copper...God's speed"

"God's speed." He slowly hung up the phone. Deep lines of pain were etched in his face. Next, he called the cab to the pizzeria address. Once again he fumbled on his pack. Using his two wrists, he picked up the pizza box and carefully squeezed

through the door. As Copper walked toward Tony's, Brogan noticed he was now limping. The evening had taken its toll on Copper's body.

As a cop, realizing the reason why Copper had bought the marijuana still had nothing to do with the fact he had broken the law. But as a human, his compassion for the man's pain and injuries made Brogan focused the camera in an entirely different direction than the pizzeria. "Maybe I should get some coffee?" Richard nodded in approval. He understood what his partner was fully saying. Brogan left the van and strolled across the street to Tony's and ordered two large coffees to go. Conveniently, he left the building just as Copper's cab pulled up to the curb. Brogan helped the old man with his belonging as he got into the back seat. Copper smiled a thank you at him.

Back in the van, Richard expressed it all in two words. "Decent coffee."

They sat quietly sipping their coffee when four men popped around the corner of the office building behind the payphone. All of them were dressed in expensive clothes— except for one. He was taller and younger than the others yet excluding his outer appearance, he seemed to fit right in. As they came within hearing distance of the microphone, the officers heard them talking about the club they had been at earlier.

"I don't think I've ever seen so many hotties in there at once. And on a Tuesday night."

"Yeah. Did you see that Adonis in the tight burgundy tank? He flirted with me all night so I finally asked him for his number and...I got it." He danced a little girlish jig. "I can't wait to screw that round hard butt of his."

"You a top? Benny, you are definitely a bottom. And you will always be a bottom until the day you die."

"So. Maybe this time I WILL be the top." His temperament turned huffy, "He doesn't know me or my past position. This might be the opportune time for me to amend my position. Maybe it's time for big changes in my life, period." They all knew when Benny said period, not to bother arguing with him. His mind was set.

"Oh, marvelous. Fluffy boys. Doesn't this just top off my night?" Richard's narrow-mindedness was showing again. He didn't understand gays and therefore had little tolerance for them.

"Don't be so old fashioned. There guys who like guys. Shut up about it already." This was the topic Brogan and Richard could never agree upon and he was too damned tired to argue with Richard about it.

"Stop babbling, you silly drunk. You always ramble on when you're drunk. Then you never do anything you say your gonna." Jeffery's own drunken wobbling had turned into body spins so he leaned against the booth to steady himself. "Why have we stopped here? I thought we going back to your place?"

Benny pointed at Ken, "He's gotta call his Mommy." He accentuated the word Mommy and ended with a mocking kissing noise.

"Hey, that's not funny. I call my Mother at least three times a week." Jeffery's dark eyes scowled down at him, "So we love our Moms. What's wrong with that?".

"Nothing. If you're a fairy," Benny teased.

"You calling me a fairy? Queer boy."

"Yes, I am. So what are you going to do about it?" He placed his scrunched up a fist in front of his friend's chin. "And I'm not a queer boy. I'm gay."

"Queer, gay, fairy. What the difference? We all still fuck guys in the ass and love it."

Ken cut in before the conversation turned into a debate about homosexuality and it's own social view about its own kind. "It'll only take a quick minute, then we can head out."

"Oh, 'head out'. Yum. That sounds delightfully arousing." He flipped his hand in the air with a phony, female gesture. He stroked himself across his chest and in his best smoldering pitched feminine voice he moaned. "Oh! Oh please hurry! I'm getting all tingly inside." It made them all laugh.

Ken stepped inside and put in his coin. The phone picked up on the second ring.

"Hello?"

His words were slightly slurred, "Hi, Mom."

"Hi, Sweetheart."

He remembered to look at his watch. "Sorry for calling you so late."

"That's all right. You know you can call me anytime."

"Mom, I'm gonna stay at Dan's tonight. I'm way too drunk to drive anywhere. That's okay, right?" He wasn't really asking for permission. He wanted her to feel like she was still an important part of his life.

"That's a good idea. Will I see you for supper tomorrow night or are you staying in the city again?" She kept it easy-going, her tone light and understanding. She didn't want him to know how much she was missing him. The apartment was so empty, so lonely without him and she needed him at home, yet she wasn't going to let him know that. He needed to be free of her guilt, to make his own decisions.

"I'm not sure? You know how it is. I'm single. My friends are single. I'll call you from work to let you know. Okay?"

"Okay." Disappointment rang through her voice. She needed to hang up before she started crying. Now he was spending most of his time in town with his new friends. She was losing her little boy. It wouldn't be long before he would meet a girl, get his own apartment and move away. Then she would be alone all the time.

"Mom. I've gotta go. The guys are waiting."

"Okay."

"Hey, Mom."

"Yeah."

"I love you."

She swallowed down the lump in her throat, "I love you too. Bye." She hung up instantly so he wouldn't hear her jagged sobs.

He said 'bye' into the buzzing phone. When he turned around, the guys had vanished. They had already drifted down the street.

Benny was admiring himself in the black mirror-like glass of the lawyer's office. He blew his reflection a flat handed kiss and screeched, "Oh you beautiful sexy beast you."

He hung up the receiver and yelled out the door. "Hey, wait for me." He darted out the doors, "Danny, wait up." The tall blonde stopped, turned, and waiting for him. He jogged to catch up to him. When he got to where he waited, Danny put his arms around his neck and kissed him on the mouth. Ken's hands slide down his back to squeeze Danny's ass. Danny threw back his head and his shrill penetrated the night air, "My virgin ass, you touched my virgin ass." With closed fists, he softly pounded Ken in the chest. "You brute. I've been violated. My virginity." They all howled at the absurdity of the words and disappeared down the alleyway.

From around the back of the van walked a petite brunette dressed all in soft pink, cinched at the waist with a thin brown belt. As she approached the booth, Brogan was able to get a shot of her shoes. Flats done in deep brown suede trimmed in pink piping and topped with tiny pink lace-up bows. Brogan smiled to himself as he pulled the camera's focus back. Richard only shook his head at his bazaar behavior. Her steps were tiny and rapid, give the impression she was a geisha girl dressed up as Gigot. When she reached the booth she swiftly pushed through the doors and lightly placed her matching mini purse on top of the phone itself. From the side pocket of her A-line skirt, she pinched out a quarter and slipped it into the slot. Careful not to break or chip a nail, she pushed in the numbers and waited for an answer. One ring, two rings...

"Hello?"

"Hi, Lynn. It's me."

"Hi, Tammy. Um...what's up?"

"Nothing."

"This is like the sixth time you've called me today. What's going on with you anyway?"

"I'm feeling kinda guilty," her words were hushed and timid.

Annoyance echoed through her friend's voice, "Oh, what did you do *this* time?"

She sounded flustered, "That's the problem. I didn't DO anything when I should have done nothing. I didn't stop myself and it was wrong, completely wrong."

"Okay, you lost me. Start at the beginning."

"You remember four nights ago when it was unbearably hot."

"Yeah."

"Well my air conditioner broke down and I had to open my bedroom window for cool air."

"So?" prodded Lynn

"It's the first time since I've lived there that I've had to open my curtain or my window at night."

"And?" Her friend's tone echoed her lack of patience.

"Oh boy, here goes, its confession time again."

"I like your confessions." Now she was interested, "So, go ahead start confessing."

Tammy inhaled deeply, "So, I was lying on my bed with the lights off. Well to be correct, I was actually at the foot of my bed so that I could get the full breeze from the open window. Then for some weird reason, I looked up and out through my bedroom window and you'll never guess what I saw."

"What?"

"In the building across from my place was my neighbor, Adrian and he was...undressing." Her voice went higher with the remembered naughty flashback. Brogan shifted forward in his chair, this interested him.

Lynn sucked in a whistle, "Whoa, naked guy. Wait, which ones Adrian? There are so many sexy guys in your neighborhood, I can't remember who's who. Describe him to me."

"He's the dark-haired Frenchman," clarified Tammy

"He's the runner, right?"

"Yep, that's him."

"Whoa again. Tell me more. Tell me everything about your Monsieur Adrian," the sound of ice clicked against a glass.

"Oh boy. He was taking off his T-shirt. I think he'd been running cause his skin was satiny with sweat. Oh God, he was breathtaking. The light reflected off every one of his taut, muscles." She let out a little squeal, "Then he started to lift weights."

"Right there in front of the open window?"

Tammy gulped some air, "Yep." In the monitor her head bobbed rapidly, "And he was facing outwards too. I guess to catch the night air like me."

"Whoa, that must have been an eyeful?"

"Oh my yes," she placed her hand flat against her hot reddening cheek. "It was an amazing sight."

"You lucky girl." The ice clinked again, "So what you do next?"

"Nothing at first."

"At first?" Lynn joked in a silly snobbish English accent, "Oh please do continue?"

"At first I laid on the bed absolutely still, so he wouldn't notice me. But after a while, I realized he was concentrating on his weight training and didn't even notice me. So I laid there motionless, watching every one of his muscles slowly stretch and flex."

"It was dark in your apartment so he wouldn't be able to see in any way." There was the sound of liquid being swallowed.

Through the van window, Brogan watched a man waiting on the sidewalk in front of the lawyer's office until she was done. He straightened his blonde ponytail in the window. Brogan had wanted to swing the camera his way but couldn't. He had to wait until she was done her conversation. The man checked his watch.

"Never thought of that. Anyway, after I realized he hadn't seen me, I kinda relaxed and um, enjoyed the show." Tammy whispered the last part out of shameful awkwardness. Her face colored deeply again while she fidgeted with the neckline of her pale pink blouse.

"That's my girl," she let out a raunchy little laugh.

In the same shy voice, she whispered, "I don't think I need to tell you what I did next."

"Please don't. That would be way more info than I need to know." There was a gulping pause, "But I don't get it, Tammy. Why are you feeling so guilty? Christ, this sorta thing happens all the time. You're so damn naïve."

Those words both insulted and infuriated her, so she challenged her friend's vicious words, "Oh yeah, you ever do it?"

"Yep. When I lived up north, there was this guy that lived in the apartment directly across and one floor down from me. I could look right down into his living room and better yet, his bathroom. He always took a shower every night before bedtime. Oh, the memories." She let out another sinful moan, "Only my 'window guy' was a blonde golf instructor. Great pecs and abs, not to mention his sweet little round rear end," The ice now rattled in the empty glass. "This would be considered kinda normal these days."

"You think so?" Tammy let out a huge sigh in the booth, "Thank God. I was worried that I was turning into a pervert or worse, a voyeur."

"A voyeur? You?" Lynn snorted loudly, "Hardly! Okay, let's verify something here. Have you watched him again since that night?"

"No!" her answer was sharp and resolute.

"Have you had the urge to look again?"

"Yeah, but I didn't. I'm having a hard enough time dealing with what I did the other night. Just that one time made me feel bad enough."

The man with the ponytail checked his watch again. Brogan wondered if he was the person of interest waiting to make the arrangements for the drug drop.

It's all good then. Now if you stood by your window every night and...well you know...enjoyed yourself, *then* you'd have a perversion. Trust me, there's no problem here. By the way, how big is he?"

"Um...I really don't know, I only saw him from the waist up, the rest of him was below the window sill."

Lynn roared with laughter, "Are you telling me that you didn't even get to see his...thingy."

She shrieked into the phone, "Good God No!!"

"Christ, my ears," Lynn barked back.

Richard wasn't prepared for it either but managed to pull his earphones away in time. Brogan wasn't so lucky and scrunched his eyes tight with pain.

"I'd died of embarrassment if I saw his...thingy."

"Holy shit, you really are a prude."

"I'm not a prude." Insulted again, Tammy was trying to hurt her with judgmental words. "Unlike you, I've got morals."

Feeling snubbed, she shot her back, "Yeah, so where was your morality four nights ago? Miss Goody Two Shoes." She slung her own barbed words.

"But that's why I'm feeling so damned guilty." She slapped her leg and stomped her foot out of frustration.

"Ah hell, guilt is way overrated. Well this kind of guilt anyway. Christ it's not like you killed someone. You just peeped at some half-naked guy." She started laughing, "Hey I just realized that this makes you a Peeping Tammy. Now that's funny!" She teased her further, "Peeping Tammy! Peeping Tammy!"

"Stop it." But her friend kept laughing. "Stop laughing at me. It's not funny!"

"Oh yes, it is!" She continued to howl with laughter, despite her friend's pleas to end the torment.

"Okay, that's it. I've had enough. Call me when you're done mocking me. You...you ..." She let out a deep grunt and slammed down the receiver. She stood in place, red-faced and fuming. "Rotten bitch!" she screamed at the phone. Angrily snatching her purse off the phone, she tore out of the booth, heading straight toward the van. Although her steps were small, they were now tiny stomps. She disappeared around the back of the van.

After Tammy had left the booth, the waiting man crossed the street with casual long strides. He went to the front of the booth but didn't go directly inside. He put in his quarter and punched in the numbers. Brogan focused on his well-worn cowboy boots. Richard ignored his partner's creepy behavior and cranked up the booth's microphone volume so they could eavesdrop on the monotone conversation.

"Hi, it's me."

"Hey. How's it going?" The woman's voice was slightly slurred, as though she had been sleeping.

"It's busy tonight." His left eye twitched and his hand tightened on the receive.

"He's lying," Brogan muttered.

"Yep," Richard caught it too.

"He's wearing the same shirt as last night and the night before that."

"Yuk."

"Oh man, his BO was so bad tonight. When I stood next to him, I thought I'd puke."

"You should say something to him. It's bad for business."

"But we've all told him. It's not just that, he smells because he doesn't shower every day. It's really gross." He flipped his ponytail over his shoulder.

"Knowing him, I can imagine."

"Tonight, was hilarious though. A female customer complained about his stench right to his face."

"Ouch! That must have been awkward? So what'd he do?"

"He turned all red and mumbled something under his breath."

Her voice was filled with sympathy, "Well hopefully he takes the hint and showers before work."

"But we both know her complaint will do no good. He's the manager and you know nothing will ever change."

"Maybe he will now that a woman has complained. You know what he's like about women? He's so lonely he'd do just about anything to get them to like him."

He stood quietly listening to her but cut in when he saw the time on his watch. "Listen, babe, I've gotta go. Stinky Boy sent me out for ice and I gotta get back. It's busy as hell tonight." His eye twitched again.

"Liar." Richard was the one to say it that time.

"Ice? Again?"

"The lazy ass bastard still didn't get the ice maker fixed. Instead he sends us out to buy ice at three times the price. What a jerk! He's gonna run the bar into the ground."

"Shit. Like I said yesterday, you better start looking for another job now before it closes. We have bills and rent to pay"

"Yeah. Like I said, it's busy tonight but I'm still thinking I should be home at the usual time. So, I'll see you in the morning." Both his eye and lower lip twitched.

Brogan laughed as he yelled, "Double liar." Richard snorted his agreement. The tension between them relaxed somewhat.

"Night. Kisses. Love you too." He hung up the phone and let out a heavy held breath. From his pocket, he pulled out another quarter and palmed it. Reaching into the back pocket of his overly tight jeans he pulled out a folded cocktail napkin and punched in the phone number.

A different female voice answered almost immediately, "Hello?"

"Hi, it's me Dallas. From the bar."

"Hi, Dallas from the bar."

"Listen, tonight you gave me your number and told me I should call you sometime. Well now is 'a sometime', right?"

She giggled in a flirty vixen voice. "It sure is, handsome."

"I'm done work and wondered if you wanted to grab a drink or something?"

"I've had plenty to drink but the 'or something' sounds like fun." She giggled again.

In the monitor, they saw his mouth drop open and then form a dirty little smile. "I was hoping for a little something myself."

"Great. My address is 171 Bell Street...Apartment D. I'll buzz you in when you get here." She lowered her voice, "Hurry...I'm waiting."

"I'm on my way."

"Byeeee."

"Byeeee." He waited until she had completely hung up, before hanging up the receiver. Bending his knees slightly, he looked downward and spoke directly to his crotch. "Here we go, Boys. Don't let me down 'cause we're getting' laid tonight."

Brogan focused in on The Boys and joked, "This guys nuts."

Richard cracked up at Brogan's double entendre. "You're fuckin' killing me, man." He wiped the tears from his eyes. Dallas left the booth and strutted back down to the alley out of sight.

FIVE

"What do we have here?" Brogan swung the camera around. "Looking lovely."

A curvy woman struts across the street, her very tight red T-shirt clinging to her shapely body and her designer jeans tapered down to her ankles. Brogan savored the red leather stiletto heels. She dug into her mini purse, pulled out a quarter and dropped it in the phone. Exhausted, she poked at the numbers. The first ring stopped halfway through.

"Hey."

"Hey," another woman repeated back

"What do you want on your pizza? Oh, come on say you want something different. Just give in this once."

"Nope. The usual. Veggies only please."

"All right, all right. Half dead animals, half-dead vegetables and covered with gooey melted cheese." She let her head slump down to rub the back of her neck. "I'm so tired tonight."

"So...how was the bar?" She already knew the answer.

"Sucked. You know, the same old shit. Nothing new happened. Dullsville. Not even a new guy to check out. Same stupid drunk people."

"Same boring crowd?"

"Yep."

"Was your 'fella' there?"

"My fella?"

"You know, that guy you've been talking about for the last week." She enjoyed teasing her, "Non-stop, all day. Yak, yak, yak. That 'fella'."

"Oh yeah, him. What a friggin' jack ass?" Her voice turned hopeless, "Christ, I thought he was something special. I was so wrong...again!"

"What? Come on, he can't be that bad?" She had hopes for her friend and this guy. It had been ages since she had a man in her life. "Enlighten me."

"Okay. Well, the gang sat together, like we always do. Only this time he sat right next to me."

"That's good, right?"

"Not really. Tonight's was the first time I talked to him one on one. Yuk and gross." She spit on the ground to back up her distaste. "Turns out, Mr. Nice Guy is actually Mr. Deviate. I found out he's into lap dances and snorting chemicals up his nose. Disgusting. I don't ever want to talk to the degenerate again." She tilted her head back against the wall and closed her eyes.

"Christ, he seemed so nice too. You never know, eh?"

"And to top it off, he starts going on and on about how 'there are slim pickings in the bar tonight'. Frig, by that time of night there only us two single girls left. Insulted the shit out of us and wasn't even smart enough know he did it. Then the jackass starts talking about this 20-year old babe he met the night before. How her tits were so damned prefect. And how she was wearing this skirt so short that it showed off her panties every time she moved in the chair. Idiotic crap like that. What bullshit? Apparently, I'm not desirable any more cause I'm over 35. What a friggin' dick head!"

"Wait a minute. He's the same age as you, but you're too old. What a fuckin' creep." She rarely swore but it made her mad to think that the asshole had hurt her friends' feelings that way. "Total fuckin' bull shit."

"Yeah, this whole evening was such a downer, that on the way here, I started to think about this aging thing. I've decided that I'm like a Christmas present."

"A Christmas present? Wow, how many shooters did you do tonight?"

"No, I mean it. Okay, you know that young-girl vs. older-woman comparison crap."

"Yeah. But nope, I'm still not following you. Why a Christmas present?"

"Ok! It's like this. On Christmas morning you run to the Christmas tree, its lights sparkling and the shiny decorations dazzling your eyes. Underneath the tree are dozens of presents and they're all for you. Some are big, some are small, others are flat and there are round ones too. Their bows are cute and perky. Their wrappings taught and wrinkle-free. Not a mark on them, no wear and tear. They are pristine. But even without unwrapping them you know what is inside the packages. You can judge what you are about to get by their shape, their color and how they sit under the tree. They are what you've longed for and there they are, just for you. You have fun opening them one by one. The hardest decision you have to make is which one to open first. Should it be the tall one wrapped in red or the petite white version? Eventually, you unwrap all the packages and find that there was only a momentary thrill in opening them, leaving you feeling disappointed and empty.

But there, in the back of the tree, you see something. That one last present you dismissed because of its outward appearance. It's not as pretty as the rest. This present has been around awhile. The wrapping paper is wrinkled, its color has faded and white spots have started to show through. Its wrapper isn't as snug as the other packages. It has an odd shape too. There are bulges in places that you wouldn't normally see them on a pretty package. The bow isn't as perky as it used to be. Time has made it sag down and flatten out.

Even though it's not as appealing as the other pretty packages, you are still drawn to that package. You can't quite figure out what's inside by its curious shape. You pick it up and listen to it. It feels different in your hands, seductive yet nurturing at the same time. The noises it makes are unique, not at all like the others. Its sound has substance. This package is exciting, almost mysterious. You open it to discover a wonderful surprise about it and about yourself. It isn't something that you would have asked for, but it is something you always wanted. You begin to enjoy the gift that was awarded to you and eventually you forget about the other pretty ones you thought you had to have. The discovery is simple, the real gift is inside and cannot be determined by its wrapper." She let out a long sigh.

"Christ, you sure know how to put it. Too bad no one else is listening."

"What can I say? That's how I feeling. I'm the present in the back." Muffling a yawn. "Anyway, I'm getting tired. I'm gonna go. Pizza's coming. See you shortly. Bye"

"No meat, only vegetarian." She got it out before the line buzzed.

She pushed her way through the doors and shuffled back across the street toward Tony's.

"That guy's an asshole? She's really pretty. I mean yeah, she not 20, but she's cute as hell. Personally, I like soft round feminine bodies." He grinned, "Besides she's got a really nice butt. Skinny girls have no butt at all. They look like little boys from behind. And look how she's dressed? She's got tons of style." Brogan focussed the camera on her in the pizza place.

"Christ, Tony sure likes her. Check out the way he's leaning into her and talking with his hands. Look. Right there. He touched her hand." Richard shook his head, "I guess she doesn't understand body language."

"Maybe she doesn't get men. How's she supposed to know that guys only touch a lady's hand if they really like them. Too bad she isn't seeing what we're seeing."

"Check out the smile on Tony's face. He's in deep."

Brogan focussed the camera on Tony's face. "Yep he's got it bad...and she's oblivious."

"Well, it's a good thing she IS oblivious to it. Christ, he's a drug dealer."

"Yeah, and considering he's getting busted tomorrow; I'd say it's the best thing."

Leon brought out the pizza and nodded hello. She put a twenty on the counter beside it. Tony held her flatten hand over his as he counted the change into her palm. He let his hands linger on hers longer than it needed to be. He flashed his eyes at her but she didn't react to his flirting. She put the change in her purse and balanced the pizza box on her hip. At the door, she turned and waved. Behind her, Tony lovingly wiggled his finger goodnight. When the door closed his shoulder slumped. She hadn't noticed him again. As she left, she almost stepped into the path of a man who definitely was in a hurry. Waiting until he passed the doorway, she stepped down onto the sidewalk and admired his butt as he walked away. Flipping her long hair behind her, she opened the blue door beside the entrance to Tony's and closed it behind her. Through the tiny window in the door, the cops watched her feet disappeared up the stairs. The light in the stairs went out. The middle window inside the apartment glowed a pale blue through its drawn sheer curtains.

As the young man rushed down the street, he flashed a quick look at himself in the lady's shop window. Abruptly, he stopped, turned completely around and headed straight toward the phone booth. He was a tall, well built, handsome man. His shoulder-length, straight auburn hair made him appear as though he should pose for 'Vogue' or be on a runway in Milan. Brogan scanned the length of his body, examining his perfectly tailored suit and ended with his brown tasseled oxfords. Richard studied Brogan for a moment but dismissed that thought immediately. By the expression on the man's face, it was plain to see that he had something weighing heavily on his mind. The lines on his forehead had distorted to deep grooves by the time he bulldozed his way through the booth's split doors. He pulled a coin out of his trouser pocket and forced it into the slot. His index finger pressed each button with determination. The phone rang only twice before someone answered.

"Hello?" Verdi opera, La Traviata, was playing in the background and Brogan tapped his fingers to the rhythm of the orchestra.

"Hi, Victor. It's me, Vinnie. "His words were said very sharp.

By the tone of his friend's voice, Victor knew something wrong. "So what's new?"

"I'm pissed off...and drunk." He ribbed his fingertip along the side of the phone. "Sorry for calling so late."

"So what happened?" Thinking, he quickly added, "That's if you want to talk about it."

"He ridiculed me again." A scowl flooded the young man's face.

"Victor's voice pitched high with disgust, "Ridiculed? I don't get it. What the hell happened this time?"

"Let's see..." Drunk, Vinnie waved his other hand in the air with excited ethnic emotions. "According to my father, his business is failing and it's all MY doing. He claims that bad things happen to him only when I'm around."

"That's ridiculous. You only reunited a few months ago."

"Eleven months," Vinnie corrected.

"So how is his business failing your fault?"

He shrugged his shoulders, "Got me. That business has been dying for years. No one is buying his so-called Italian suits anymore. Not since that rumor went around town."

Victor quickly spoke up, "I still can't believe that about him. He doesn't seem the type to mess with little girls."

Brogan sat up straight in his chair. "You hear that?"

"Yep." Richard pulled his notepad closer, poising his pen ready to write down any details they heard.

Vinnie was quiet for a few moments before his tactfully reply. "You do know I was sent away to my Aunt Maria's when I was eight?

Victor rambled off the reason everyone in the neighborhood knew about. "Because your Mother died and your father worked too much to take care of you."

Vinnie cut him off, "No. That wasn't the reason." He stood silent, trying to figure out how to say the next part. He decided it was best to just come out with the truth. "I found out I was sent away for my own protection. From my father."

His voice jolted to higher-pitched, "What? That's news to me and I've known your family for years."

"Auntie Maria told me they worried he would try to do to me what he did to some of the other little kids in my family."

"Other kids?" There was still wavering in Victor's voice.

"Maria said it was mostly touching. But the family worried about me with my mother no longer there to watch out for me. Concerned he would escalate from touching to more perverted assaults." The gasp on the other end of the phone told him he had finally made Victor understand the seriousness of the accusations. "She couldn't bring herself to say the word molestation out loud but I know that's what she was implying he might do to me. Cousins confirmed what she had told me."

"I've never seen this part of him."

"Why do you think it took me this long to reunite with him? I'm now old enough that I'm safe from his sexual advances. If he touched me now, I'd punch his head in."

"So that's why. We wondered why you never accepted his invitation to come for the holidays. Now that I think about it that explains a lot of things between you and father."

"Sure does...but it doesn't explain why he's treating me like shit now. I mean, he ridiculed me in front of Gina. And you know everyone in the neighborhood will hear about that."

"Oh, Christ. Telephone...telegraph...tell Gina."

Vinnie groaned, "Tell me about it."

"So what was the problem? What did you supposedly do to make Mario yell at you?"

"I suggested that Gina buy a tan-colored tie to go with the blue shirt she was buying for Marco."

"And?"

"Mario had put a raspberry red tie on top of it and was trying to convince Gina in to buy it."

"No, no. That's not a good combination. Why would he do that? Has he gone color blind all of a sudden?"

"No, but he over ordered raspberry ties and needed to unload them. Cheap bastard won't pay the 35% restocking fee so he's pushing them on every guy that comes in the shop."

"Sounds like him." He chuckled, "What did tell Gina to make her think bright blue and raspberry went together?"

"That it's the latest fashion in New York." Vinnie snorted, "So I asked him what part of Mew York ...the Bronx?" He laughed again, "He didn't find that funny at all."

"I bet." Victor laughed along with him.

"Gina got the hint and asked for a different tie. A tan tie."

"Oh, oh."

"Yep. And Mario being Mario, decided to make me look like as idiot so he could unload a stupid ugly tie."

"Jesus, what did he say?"

"He went on and on about how I didn't know anything about clothing because I ran out on the family business, leaving him to run everything by himself." Vinnie's finger angrily drummed the top of the phone, his voice cold. "He was yelling it straight in my face. Almost nose to nose. Gina got very quiet. Very scared. She backed out the front door as fast as she could to get away from him. That's when he got really mean. Started blaming me for everything. His failing business. His girlfriend leaving him. His miserable life." By the end, he was yelling in the receiver.

Holding the phone away from his ear, Victor's voice was faded, "Sounds like Mario. Seriously, Vinnie, he had no right to treat you that way. You don't need to put up with that kind of abuse."

"I know, I know. He's a jerk." There was a silent pause. "But he's still my father."

Victor put as much sympathy as he could in voice, "Honestly Vinnie, no one would blame you if you didn't want him in your life."

"I'm beginning to understand that."

There was a long silence between them. In the background of the phone, an alarm clock went off. "That's me. Time to get ready for work. Kitchen prep waits for no one." There was a loud SMACK, making the alarm stop buzzing. "Listen, come into the restaurant this afternoon. We need to talk about this. I'm here for you Vinnie."

"Sounds good. And I should be sober by then too." They both chuckled at that statement.

"It's a plan then. I'll see you…"

Over his words, Vinnie blurted out, "Are the rumors true, Victor? Is my father a pervert?"

He said his words carefully. "As long as I've known Mario, he has never been charged with molestation."

"That's not what I'm asking you." He squeezed his eye tight, hoping Victor's answer wasn't what he feared. "Did Mario DeLuca hurt children?" The silent pause on the end of the phone spoke volumes in Vinnie's ears.

With a sharp sigh, Victor broke his silence. "I didn't want to talk about this over the phone. In-person, you and me, we will talk about what I know."

Richard threw his pen across the room. "Damn it!"

Brogan tried to calm him, "We got a name and a suit business. That's a good place to start."

The tension was back, two-fold.

Vinnie pinched the bridge of his nose to ease the pain building behind his eyes. "That's what I was afraid of."

Victor whispered the words, "The truth won't be easy...for either of us." Another painful pause hung between them. "Look, you come to the restaurant and we'll talk. A serious talk. But first, you get some sleep and sober up. You want tortellini? You know Sophia makes the best in town."

Vinnie laughed, "Food is always a cure for you."

"Hey, you gotta eat." The alarm buzzed again. He cleared his throat, "Listen, I gotta go. The guys will be waiting in the back alley for me to let them in the kitchen. But you come today. We will talk."

"Yes, yes. Will do. Ciao Victor."

"Ciao, Figlio."

The phone buzzed in his hand as he stood there looking at the van. He hung up the receiver but continued to look at the van. Brogan focussed in on his face.

"Why's he looking at us?"

"Damned if I know? Wait, back it up some. He's doing some with his hands."

Vinnie reached inside his jacket front pocket and pulled out something long and black.

Richard yelled, "Gun."

"No, it's not. It's a note pad," Brogan pulled the camera back. He poked fun at Richard, "Oh my god, he's got a loaded note pad and pointy a pen. Save me from the bad man, you big hunk of a cop."

Vinnie put the opened note pad against the glass wall of the booth and clicked the pen with his thumb. Brogan focussed in closer on the page. Vinnie looked back over his shoulder toward the van. Back and forth, his long ponytail swishing each time.

"He's writing down the phone number from the side of our van. What'a shmuck? Look at what he's writing."

The note on the monitor read, 'Peter's Plumbing - Industrial/Commercial/Residential 1-800-FIX-PIPE'. Off to the side, he scribbled out the corresponding numbers after checking the letters on the phone's keypad. Below it, he carefully printed, - CALL TUES. RE: DOWNSTAIR LADIES WASHROOM.

Richard snickered, "Wait 'til he calls it and reaches the front desk at the precinct. Dave will put him through the wringer. He'll give up in no time."

Brogan softly repeated, "Yeah, what'a shmuck?" By the attitude in his voice, Richard wondered if Brogan was a little jealous of Vinnie's good looks and fabulous clothing.

Vinnie tucked the note pad back inside his jacket and left the booth. They watched him retrace his steps before and disappeared down the alley.

Over the radio came the call Richard had been waiting for. Pam had left her apartment and was at the Western Union picking up her money. The worry lines on Richard's face softened once he knew she safely out of her apartment and away from Mitch the abuser.

They sat watching the monitors for any signs of life. In the monitor Richard watched the blue light of the apartment window go out. All the sounds of the street had faded and the quiet it brought made Brogan restless and uneasy. Deciding to start some of the night's paperwork as a distraction and he began sorting out the sheets into separate piles. Again the crackling sound of the pages being shuffled back and forth irritated Richard, his quick huff and glance in his partner's direction filling the van with more tension.

Rubbing the eraser end of his pencil along his note pad out of boredom, Richard finally asked, "You want coffee or tea? It's my turn to get coffee."

"Tea. Coffee at this time of night sits too heavy on my guts." Brogan squared the ends of the last paper stack.

"Orange pekoe, black oolong or earl grey?"

"No fancy-ass teas for me. Good old ordinary orange pekoe is all I need."

He couldn't resist the slam. Word for word he quoted Brogan's alfalfa sprouts insult. 'Just try 'em, picky pants. You might even LIKE something NEW for once."

"Yuk, yuk, yuk." He swung the camera up and down the street. "Actually, I've tried many types of teas from different parts of the world. For your information, one of the ladies I dated was a tea importer. We always enjoyed tea after we enjoyed each other." He smirked at his partner, "I still prefer my ordinary orange pekoe though." Brogan won that round and they both let it go.

"You need milk for it?" He remembered that cream was not a friend of Brogan's lower digestive system.

He pointed over his shoulder with his thumb, "Um, look in the mini-fridge first. Henderson might have left some in there. He's a milk drinker."

Richard rolled his chair over to the fridge and yanked open the door. "Yep, there's milk. There's peanut butter, cheese and a loaf of bread too."

"All right, snacks."

"No fuckin' way. If it's Henderson's, we'll never hear the end of it. Shit, he still bitches about the lemon filled doughnut I ate during the Cassidy stakeout."

"Christ, that was over a year and a half ago?"

"Yep. He's a tightwad."

Brogan thought to himself, 'If that isn't the pot calling the kettle black'. He turned his head away from his partner to hide his amusement.

Richard walked toward the back door, "What's so damned funny?"

"Nothing."

"Like fuck it's nothing." He opened the sliding door and fresh clear night air rushed in, replacing the stale, thick, musty air.

"A guy could die of thirst around here." Brogan made a choking sound while clasping his throat, "Cough, cough, cough."

"Fuck off!"

With a laugh, brogan shot back, "No problem. After I drink my tea, I'll get right on it."

Standing squarely in the open doorway, Richard gave him a double-finger-salute, jumped to the sidewalk and loudly slammed the door shut. Brogan followed h m with the camera. Stopping on the opposite sidewalk Richard scratched his butt with his middle finger before going into SPOONS. After Tommy took his order, the cop scurried to the rren's room. Tommy vanished into the kitchen and returned a few minutes later with two small flat white takeout bags. He carefully placed them in with the hot tea. Richard paid him and cautiously slid the cardboard tray off the counter. Heading back toward the van he walked up the street, crossed by the payphone, walked passed the front of the van and slipped into the door. He took the different return route to throw off anybody that might be watching.

"You still like cinnamon toast or is your palate too refined for such simple fare?" He tossed the flat bag at him.

"Cinnamon toast! I fuckin' love cinnamon toast. Always reminds me of my Mom."

"Yeah, me too."

Out of a cab slinks a statuesque beauty. Brogan recognizes the long Latin legs immediately. She entered the coffee shop to a smiling Tommy, who made her coffee and took her money. It irritated Brogan to watch the coffee boy gawking at her ass when she walked out the door and across the street.

"That's Lolita from accounting." Brogan crumpled up the white bag and pitched it in the wastebasket. He forced himself to casually comment, "Girl's got class."

'Better than that, she's got brains. She knew exactly how to fix my screwed up paycheque. Last month they charged me twice for my pension deduction. Lolita made three phone calls, did some computer work and Ta-Dah, all fixed." Richard's curiosity was triggered by the expression on Brogan's face. He wiped the cinnamon crumbs off his lips and slurped on his hot tea. He decided a little investigation work was in order. "How long has she been working upstairs?"

"She started in 1990." He added another half packet of sugar to his tea.

Richard swallowed his last mouthful of toast. "Wow. Good memory."

"Not really. That's the year I got in all that trouble. She was the 'new girl' in accounting and got stuck handling my pay problems. She stayed with me through the whole thing though. Yep, she's a goddess." Brogan followed her with the camera as she stepped onto the black shiny asphalt.

"She married?" Richard the match-maker was at it again. He thought Brogan and Lolita would make a good-looking couple And her choice of footwear was just Brogan's type. Fashionable and sexy.

"Nope."

He scrunched up his white bag and ricocheted it off Brogan's head, "What? You getting lazy or something? What's stopping you? Ask her out."

He tried hard to keep his voice casual, "Who says I haven't?"

"Well? Fill me in buddy."

"She said no." Brogan blew on his tea, hoping to hide his raw, wounded emotions.

"So she said no. Wait. Don't tell me you gave up on the first try?"

"Nope. She said no nine times altogether. She said she doesn't date people that she works with. It's a personal policy of hers." He tossed his pen across his desk. "You know what? I think her policy sucks shit."

This was it. The exact moment that Richard had been anticipating all night and he went for it. "Well, she probably did you a favor anyway." The words were casually presented with a touch of pity, so as to not trigger his partner's keen sense of deception.

"What'd ya mean?" Brogan took the bait.

"Well, think about it. She'd start dating you and you'd get all 'love in the pants' for her, right?" Richard was trying not to laugh.

"Yeah, so?" Brogan scanned her body from head to toe. Brogan grinned at the sight of the tapered kitten heels on her glossy black mules. His hands were sweating.

"Then she'd find out what kind of weirdo you really are and run away screaming."

Brogan shot him an intense look before throwing his note pad at his head, "Fuck you, Dick Head."

Richard tossed it back. "Christ, take a joke, will ya?" Brogan was taking this too seriously and to Richard, that meant there was a powerful problem inside his partner. Brogan kept things inside until they devoured him, mind and soul.

"Shut up. She's in." Under his breath, he called Richard a Dick Head again.

She tried to ease the handle of her purse off her shoulder but it got tangled with the thick strap of her silky black dress. The strap slipped down, exposing the rich olive skin of her shoulder. Brogan focussed the camera on the nape of her slender neck.

"Christ Brogan. What are you doing? This is on tape. Knock it off."

"She's perfect." His soft voice revealed the agonizing passion he held for her. It had been a long time since he felt that way about another woman. His wife had been the love of his life and when she died, he didn't think anyone could make him feel that way again. Lolita made him ache.

"Let it go, Brogan. Let it go." Richard realized that his partner was completely infatuated by her. Brogan's past obsessions had gotten him into deep trouble and this one worried him as well. "She's just a girl. There are a lot more out there. Honest, I've seen them." His attempt at humor was wasted.

Brogan pounded his fist on the desk and shot him another angry glare. "Shut the fuck up. It's ringing. And I want to hear who she's calling." He was almost growling the words.

Richard froze. His partner behavior was not only inappropriate, his quickly flipped demeanor was scary.

While she waited, Lolita blew on her coffee with her full ruby lips. She motioned to hang up when somebody picked up.

"Hello?" A soft sleepy female voice answered

"Hi. It's me." Lolita kissed the edge of the cup against her cheek.

"What time is it?"

"I want to come over." Her tone changed to a sultry whisper. "Please, I need you tonight. I can't stand being away from you this long. Please, I need to be with you."

From the corner of his eye, Richard watched his partner's reaction carefully, preparing for a violent outburst. But Brogan didn't move. Truth was, he was in shock.

With a giggle, she teased Lolita, "Persuade me."

"Persuade you?" She teased back, "I'd love to."

"Convince me. Tell me what you're going to do when you get here."

Lolita enjoyed this part of the game, "When get there I'm hoping that the door won't be locked, so I can sneak into the bedroom and ravish your naked hot body."

Brogan's head fell forward slightly. His heart silently crushed in his chest. He did his best to kept his emotions from showing on his face. The last thing he needed was pity from Richard.

"Yum. Tell me more. Details, I want details."

"Demanding aren't you?" Lolita sipped her coffee while she gathered her thoughts. "First, I imagine that you're wearing that little black teddy I gave you at Christmas."

Richard heard Brogan hopelessly whisper, 'Christmas.'

"The silky one or the lacy one?"
"Yes, the silky one. I love the way your tits feel when they are cover in silk. Next, I'm gonna kiss you all over your..."

Brogan couldn't take any more. He turned everything off. He sat there, very quiet, almost crippled by the pain. After exhaling a deep breath to ease the suffering, he spoke up, "It'll be on the tape. She doesn't deserve to have her personal life plastered all over the station. You should erase it now. Tell me when she's gone...please." The last word was a plea of compassion for his breaking heart.

"Okay." Richard's sympathy went out to him. There were no jokes this time, only mercy. "Hey Bro. Sorry, buddy."

Brogan shrugged his shoulders. "I didn't know." He closed his eyes to stop himself from looking at her. He concentrated on his breathing, trying to stop tears from forming in his eyes.

"No one knew. Don't beat yourself up over this. There'll be others."

In the silence, Richard waited until she was completely out of sight before telling him to start the camera again. Brogan tried to push Lolita out of mind by focussing the camera on the young boy in the coffee shop.

From inside SPOONS, a teenage boy wearing all white dashed across the street and over to the booth. He slipped in his coin and pecks each button. He impatiently tapped his fingers on the top of the phone. It rang only once before it's picked up.

"Hi, Sweet-ums! How's your night?"

"I miss you sooo much Nicky!" The girl's voice pined for him.

"I miss you more," he teased back.

"No, I miss you more," she giggled.

"No, I miss you even more."

Richard loathed these sickening phone calls. "Holy fuckin' Christ. Save me from this shit." He had two daughters and endured many of these annoying conversations in their early teenage years. His screechy mocking voice came automatically, "No, I wuss you more. No, I wuss you a hundred times more."

Brogan, trying to forget the pain of Lolita's call, joined in the gag. Humor cures all. "No, I wuss you all the way to the moon."

Richard placed his clasped hands under his chin and batted his eyes at Brogan. "No, I wuss you so much I could die."

"No, no, I'll wuss you 'til the end of time."

As the couple expressed their 'undying love' for each, a stocky middle-aged man passed between the booth and the camera.

"I can't talk long, I'm replacing Tommy, he's gotta leave early tonight. He going to some boring birthday party with that airhead girlfriend of his. That girl's eleven doughnuts short of a dozen."

"Hey, that's not nice. I've met her and she's kinda sweet." Nicky's insults worried her. "I hope you don't talk about me like that?"

"No baby, I love you. You're smart and you're beautiful and you're sexy and...damn I miss you."

"Oh, I miss you too," she gushed back.

"Not as much as I miss you."

With his emotions still raw, Brogan couldn't stand it. "Oh, Christ. Not again." He turned down the volume until they were barely audible. "It's times like this that I realize the force doesn't pay me enough money to endure this kinda cruelty."

"You think this is bad? Try listening to this shit coming out of your own daughter's mouth." He rolled his eyes, "Every friggin' night. Usually right in the middle of some important hockey game or something. Made me want to puke." He picked up his pen and started scribbling, "Let's see...two daughters...fifteen calls per week...for two years. Umm, that works out to be...6240 of these sickening conversations. Nauseating, completely nauseating."

"Listen, I gotta go. Tommy's pacing like lunatic in the coffee shop. He wants to get going. I'll call you before school tomorrow. Okay?"

"Yeah, okay. I'm gonna really miss you 'til then."

"I'm gonna miss you more."

"No, I'm gonna miss you more," her voice was high pitched and sickly sweet.

Brogan stuck his finger partway in his mouth and made a vomiting sound. Richard groaned in unison.

"Baby, I gotta go, Tommy's waiting."

"Yeah, I love you Sweet-ums! I talk to you in the morning."

"Goodnight Baby."

"Goodnight Sweet-ums."

"Goodnight."

"Goodnight."

She teased, "You hang up first."

"No. You hang up first," he teased back.

"No. You hang up first."

"You throw up first." Brogan started this round of mockery.

"No. You throw up first," Richard whined like a girl.

"No. You throw up first."

"No. I want to throw up more." his gagging noises were comic genius.

"No. I want to throw up more." They both convulsed with laughter.

"You hang up first." In the booth, Nick was rolling his eyes. Even he was getting fed up with the cutsie stuff.

"Let's hang up at the same time," she sounded very serious about this, "Okay?"

"Okay, on the count of three." It was obvious he was playing along just to get away from her.

"Okay."

"One...two...three...bye." He didn't wait for the silly game this time, he hung up right away. Nick sprinted back to SPOONS. Inside, the stocky man was sitting on a stool waiting for his order. Tommy chucked his apron under the counter, ran out the door and disappeared down the alley.

"It's over," Brogan put his palms together and prayed to the ceiling, "Thank you, Lord!"

"Hey, who's the guy in the coffee shop? He looks familiar." Richard had a weird feeling about the guy. His lawman's sixth sense was triggered.

"Beats me?" Brogan focussed closer on his face. "Wait. He DOES look familiar."

"Give me a minute." Richard squinted his eyes and turned his head sideways. "I got it! That's Handgun Harley."

"Can't be? The last time I saw Handgun Harley, he weighed over three hundred pounds, with long greasy hair and one of the mangiest beard I've ever seen. Even for a biker."

Richard pointed at the screen, "Look closer. There, in the eyes. And check out his left wrist. 'HELLBOUND' in red blood dripping letters. He got that tattoo just before he went into the Pen for Old Man Langley's murder. It's him all right and I bet you five bucks, he's our drug man."

"You're right about the eyes, but ten bucks says you're wrong on drug thing. Harley's never been connected to the drug scene. He's a killer by trade. Remember that massive tattoo on his chest, DEATH FOR DOLLARS?"

"Unless he's started a new profession." He hoped the betting would take Lolita off his mind. "You're on. But let's make it an even fifty bucks."

Brogan whooped. "Game on!" He pulled out a pair of twenties and a ten. Richard yanked a fifty from his wallet. Both of them put their 50 dollars on the desktop between them.

On the monitor they watched Harley pay Nick for his order and head out the door. He shuffled the containers in his massive arms and crossed the street toward the booth. Inside the booth, he carefully placed the food order on the floor to make his phone call. One ring, two rings...

An angry woman thundered, "Harley, you lazy bastard. Where in the hell are you? You're late...again. You better not have been drinking with your asshole buddies again. 'Cause if you have Harley, look out."

Brogan cranked the volume down before his ears drums exploded. Grinning he reached for the money.

But Richard stopped him, "Not yet. He's not finished." He let his earphone drop to rest on his neck.

"No. I worked an extra half-shift at work."
"You better not be lying to me."

"No, I'm not lying. And I picked up some snacks for you. I hope apple pie is all right?" The big man's voice was timid, almost to the point of being pathetically apologetic.

"Apple? I hate fuckin' apple pie. Can't you do anything right? You're so fuckin' stupid. Why do I put up with you? Come home. Right now."

The officers weren't sure if it was out of submission or shame but Handgun Harley lowered his head as he said the word, "Okay."

"What was that?"

"Yes Ma'am," he quickly corrected.

"That's better." She let out a heavy sigh that rushed through their headsets. "You better be here in fifteen minutes or there'll be hell to pay." During her mean streaks, she had become predictable making Harley pulled the receiver away from his ear to avoid the loud clatter that he knew was coming. His big hand returned the receiver gently to its cradle.

He mocked her words out loud, "There'll be hell to pay." He scrunched up his face. "You're so fuckin' stupid." He yanked the food off the floor and shoved the doors open. "Fuckin' bitch. One of these days, I'm not coming back, you'll see." He looked into the night sky and mumbled, "Fuck my life sucks!" His shoulders slumped. Handgun Harley had become a whipped man and he knew it. As he passed in front of the van, he looked directly into the window and gave an enormous friendly grin. It was as though he knew they were there watching him.

Richard jerked straight up in his chair, "Christ. That was spooky."

Brogan was outright rattled. "Where did he go? Is he gone? " He blasted his chair to the back window and peered through the heavily smoked glass. Richard stood between the front seats and watched as Handgun Harley's silhouette disappeared around the corner. "He's gone."

"Do you think he knew we were here? He's been around enough busts that he might have seen a look-a-like van. Maybe we should call this in and see what the Captain wants to do?" Brogan was speed blabbing and turning pale, "You're sure he's gone?"

Richard had never seen Brogan so shook up. "Christ, what's with you. You look like you've seen a ghost. Calm down, ya big baby."

"Fuck you! Two years ago, me and Forman were watching an apartment over on the eastside. Forman went for coffee and a piss break. The exact same thing happened there. Only that guy walked over to his car and pulled a three-foot crowbar from his backseat. I watched him walk straight to the window in front of me. His eyes had that wild far off lunatic gaze while he started smashing the glass in. And the whole time he's yelling, 'Here piggy, piggy...here piggy, piggy.' The bastard got through too." Brogan lifted his shirt to expose a knot of thick scars. "Fucker impaled me repeatedly before Forman got back. One shot in the shoulder. That's all it took to slow him down enough for Foreman to cuff him." He closed his eyes and swallowed hard. "Okay, the crowbar didn't go completely through my

Kevlar vest each time, but it still did damage." He rifted his shirt back around his belt, "So calm down, my ass. Is he gone or not?"

"Yeah, he's definitely gone."

"Sure?" He was still anxiously looking out the window.

"I swear on my unborn grandchild."

Brogan let out a held breath and let his shoulders relax, "Okay, now I'll calm down." He grabbed the hundred dollars off the desk, jammed it in his pocket and sat down hard in his chair.

Richard didn't complain like he normally would have. He had something on his mind. "Is that why I didn't see you around the precinct for a while?"

"Yeah. Three weeks in the hospital and another week at home. Then the Captain put me on desk duty for another month. I thought I'd fuckin' go insane."

Richard walked back to his desk. "Oh yeah, now I remember. That was around the same time my Mom passed away."

"Your Mom passed away?" Brogan turned in his chair to face him, "Oh shit, I didn't know that. Sorry, nobody told me. Well...they might have but I was on so many pain killers that I might have not understood. I was really doped up for awhile. Man, I'm really sorry. She was a great lady. I loved those goody bags she used to send you in the winter. Those sugar cookies that melted like butter in your mouth. What kinda tea did she send? Earl Grey? Yeah, Earl Grey. Sorry I missed the funeral." This was definitely another reason for the awkwardness between them.

"She died in her sleep. Leave it to my Mom to pass away with no fuss to anybody." He opened his notebook. "I looked for you at the wake. I was hoping you'd show up. I hadn't seen you in so long." Richard hung his head and coodled on the pad. "I thought you were still angry with me. Sure could've used my friend there."

"I swear Richie, I didn't know or I would have been there. Pissed off or not, I would have been there I loved your Mom too. You know that. She was a fine lady."

Richard swallowed down the lump in his throat, "We've got company." He watched Brogan's body tensed up again. "Relax. It's a woman." He inhaled slowly, releasing the tight tension in his chest. 'Don't cry. Jesus fuck sakes, don't cry.' he repeated in his head.

From down the street, there came a short square woman. She stomped straight to the booth. In went her quarter. One ring...two...three...

"Hello?"

"Hello." She blew out a long slow breath.

"Morag? What's wrong?" Glenna had heard that heavy sigh before, she'd been crying.

Her voice cracked. "Nottin'."

"Oh, Jesus? What'd ta drunken arsehole do t'is time?"

"Arsehole...you mean chanty wrassler." She turned angry. "Tanight makes one hundred. I'll take no more of his shite."

"Lewis no hit you, did he?" She had always worried about that happening. Some Scottish would men turn mean when they drank.

"Naw. He be to friggin' snookered. Daftie, t'at all."

"What tales is he tellin' now?"

"Ya gonna love t'is one," even she laughed at the stupidity of the situation. "Accordin' to him it's his right as a Scotsman ta drink himself blootered."

"Naw. Yah be foolin' me?"

"Aye. Lewis believes t'at he's a Scotsman and t'at it be a true tradition for him to go the pub for 'a pint or two' like his Da and Gran Da."

"Ya not sayin' he t'inks it's an ancestral right?"

"Aye. Glenna t'at what I'm a sayin'."

"Holy lifting Jesus, he's finally gone bampot. Ancestral right, my arse. Aye, what be t'is shite about him bein' Scottish? How many friggin' years has he bin here?"

"His kin fled Scotland when he was eight. So t'at's...29 years past."

"T'at's mincing it a bit now isn't it?" Glenna was filled with contempt for his lies.

"Not to him. In his mind, he's still Scottish t'rough and t'rough." In the booth, she shook her head at her own disbelief in him.

"Jesus. Ta only thin' Scotch about him is his accent...and ta whiskey in his gut."

"Arsehole. Auld numpty. Stupid drunken arsehole."

Glenna once had a distinct Welch accent of her own but had lost most of it over the years. She only talked the old language around Morag. "What about ta accent? He's been here 29 years and he's no lost it yet?"

"Naw. His Maw is here enough t'at her accent keeps his agoin'."

"True. Your Maw and you are da same too."

"Aye but I'm no usin' it as an excuse to drink meself blootered. Ya had to see him, outright fuckult. Absolutely drunk. Slurring his words. And stink, smelt like he shite his kinkers."

"Oh Morag, has he gotten' t'at clatty?"

"Howfin he is and he's been t'at way for 100 days in a row. I've counted t'em on the calendar. Friggin' fool." Morag grunted through her teeth. "Aye and I'll take no more."

"What are ya goin' to do t'en?"

"Shoot the crow. Be soon enough too. But I need ta save some silver for a flat of me own."

"Bunk with me."

"Oh no, I can't be a bother to ya."

"I no mind. True. Ya helped me when Bernie passed on. A debt paid. Let me help ya. Stay here. At least for tanight."

Morag went silent.

"Come on t'en, just for tonight," she prodded.

"Oh, right t'en. 'Sides I no wanna go home to t'at drunken arse."

"Braw. T'at be a good lassie. Where are ya? I'll come get ya."

"Cross from Tony's Pizza. I'll wait t'ere for ya."

"Be t'ere in right direct."

"Ter-rah." She hung up the phone and headed to Tony's. Brogan followed her with the camera.

"Morag, you poor girl," was Brogan only comment.

Baffled, Richard needed some clarification. "Do you have any idea what the hell they said?"

"Yep. Understood every word. I'm part Scottish. My Mom's family is Half Scotch and half Irish."

"And you understood all that gibberish?"

"Yep."

"Great. So what did they say?"

"Basically, Morag's husband is your typical Scottish drunk and that he will never amount to anything in life because of it. She's finally had enough and thinks she wants to leave him. In the meantime, she gonna staying at Glenna's." Brogan snatched up his pen. "But she wasting her time 'cause he'll persuade her to come back with great promises of renewed sobriety." He scribbled a few numbers in his notebook. "You see, all Scottish men have great powers of persuasion when it comes to making women believe things. Things they would normally consider ridiculous. Eventually, he'll deny he ever said it and if he did say it, he never really meant it or worse, blame it on the booze, saying it was the whiskey talking. Then ultimately it'll be her fault for even listening to him in the first place. She'll be nothing but a silly, foolish female who doesn't know what the hell she's talking about. I've seen it all too many times. Christ, it's happened in my own damned family."

"Okay but what the hell is a chanty wrassler? Did I say it right?"

"Close enough. It's a Scottish term. I think it means a 'useless dishonest person'."

Richard scoffed, "Hey that reminds me of a joke. Why did God invent whiskey?" He paused like he was a comedian, "Because she did want the Scots to rule the world." Richard chuckled to himself.

"That's an old one. I've got one for ya. Why did the Scotsman cross the road?"

Richard shrugged.

"Because the pub on the other side had larger pints." It was Brogan's turn to laugh by himself.

"I don't get it. It's really not that funny."

"I guess it's only funny if you're a Scotsman." He panned across the street to where Morag was waiting outside Tony's.

SIX

A slim man in a simple black suit appeared from behind the van. Instantly both the officers realized him as a man of the cloth. The priest watched as a young couple passed by on the other side of the street. He waited outside the booth until they were gone. He studied Morag as she left Tony's and recognized that she was more concerned about herself than about anything he was doing. He nervously pulled something from his jacket pocket. Studying the item he hid in his palm, he calmed himself with a long deep breath, then casually strolls to the booth.

Once inside, he lowered his head and prayed softly out loud. "Forgive me Lord for what I'm about to do, for I know it is forbidden. Please understand that it helps me cope with it all. All the baptisms of children, when I'm denied the right to have children of my own. Performing weddings when I can never marry. The young beautiful virgins that complete their confirmation before me each spring. The morbid deaths of funerals and wakes, that haunt me. I need this. It is the only thing that keeps me alive inside. Heavenly Father, please forgive me for my sins. Amen." He lifted his head and opened

his eyes. Taking one last penetrating breath, he placed the call.

Brogan focussed the camera on the keypad and howled, "It's a 1-900 number."

"A sex line? Holy Christ." Richard couldn't believe it.

The pre-recorded message came on after one ring, "You have reached 'Heavenly Voices'. The following is for adults only, 19 years of age or older. Please be advised that your call will cost $2.99 per minute. To help guide you with your call a 'Heavenly Voices' representative will be with you shortly. Please have your credit card ready. Thank you for calling 'Heavenly Voices'."

"Good evening, will this be on your 'Heavenly Voices' account or is this a credit card purchase?"

"It's on my card." He swallowed down his guilt hard. It wasn't his card. He had found it on the floor of the confessional booth. He intended to use it only the one time and then return it. Mr. Paul Smitherson's confession was a tantalizing adventure for the priest. The man told of his sexual conversation with a real live woman, a woman Paul couldn't touch. It was the perfect solution to the holy man's problem; his problem of loneliness and deep sexual cravings. The priest decided that Mr. Paul Smitherson was a rich man that could afford to pay for his sex calls too. And after all, who was the sinner going to tell without getting himself in trouble.

The taped voice was a mixture of fake sweetness and monotony, "Using your touch-tone phone, please enter your credit card number now."

He punched the numbers into the phone and slipped the card into his jacket pocket. The numbers peeped through their computer system.

"Thank you, sir. Is there someone in particular you'd like to speak with this evening?"

He cut in quickly. "Yes. I'd like to speak with Jezebel, please." His heart rate sped up as he said her name.

"I'll see if she available sir. Please hold?" Sleazy electronic music pulsated in the receiver. For him, it was taking an eternity.

"Jezebel is available...just for you sir." She added the required sweet talk in a monotone voice, "I will put you through now. Thank you and we appreciate your business." The same dreadful porn music played while he waited.

"Jezebel...good stage name."

"Yeah, if you're going to be a phone whore, naming yourself after one of the most infamous bible bitches, would work well."

A car pulled up in front of Tony's. "There's Glenna." Brogan thought to himself, 'Good luck Morag, you'll need it.'

"Hi, this is Jezebel." Her voice forced soft and feminine to please the client on the other end of the phone.

"Jezebel save me from this torment."

"Father is that you?" She had served him many times before and just assumed that the priestly image was part of his fantasy.

"Yes, my child, it is me." Both relief and excitement filled him at the exact same time, adding to the anticipation of the call.

"Oh Father, I have been waiting for your call. You make me so happy when we talk. I feel delivered from my wretched life after we converse." She made the extra effort for this client. He talked for a long time and that meant good money for her. The longer the call, the higher the charges, and that meant a bigger percentage for her.

"My child. What would you like to talk about this evening?" It was his little trick to get her to initiate the start of the dialog.

It was her job to know her clients' needs and desires. She flipped through her Rolodex to refresh her memory. The information on the card described his preferences, written in red felt marker. She read the list from the card in her head; innocent child; old language; the third notation was smeared but she knew what it had once read. "The wanton lusts of Sodom and Gomorrah. Tell me what happened in those cities that made God so angry."

"No Jezebel, tonight I'd like you to tell me what you believed happened so long ago. Describe each sin to me so I may be sure you fully understand how terribly immoral they truly were." His pulse began to race, tension swelled in his chest.

Jezebel was a master at her craft and she switched her voice to that of an angelic child. The card told her it was what he desired as a client. "Well, let me see. I imagine that many of the women enjoyed fornicating. Most women fornicated with one man at a time, but some of the harlots might have wanted to fornicate with more than one man at a time. That's very bad, isn't it Father?"

"Yes, that's very bad." He closed his eyes to visualize the scene in his mind.

"I mean, one woman laying in bed with a man at each end of her. She's a wicked woman, isn't she Father?"

He whispered it, "Yes. Wicked."

"Imagine she has man's penis inside her while she has another in her mouth. She's a godless whore." Jezebel emphasized the word whore. She could tell by his heavy breathing it was turning him on. As blood rushed to his groan, his hands began to sweat.

'Oh, Father. What if another woman wanted to join them? Just the thought of the four of them engaging in perverted fornicating. It's shameful, an indecent image. The two women giving themselves eagerly to strange savage men, opening their legs and exposing themselves. Making them want to put their penises into their warm wet vaginas. Those whores would probably want to fornicate with each other too. Rubbing each other breasts until they were swollen firm and plump with big hard nibbles. They'd want to lick and suck on them too. Wouldn't they Father?"

"Oh...yes...they...would." He was breathing so heavily, he could barely talk.

"Oh, and the men. I think they'd touch themselves while they watched those whores put their fingers inside each other. Their sin-filled moaning and screams of depraved delights would fill the room."

The priest sucked air over his teeth. That sound told her she was doing her job well tonight. "Tell me more of these...sins."

"Father, what would happen if the men wanted to fornicate with both whores at the same time? My mind imagines the two couples watching each other fornicating. Why it's dirty, just dirty. Hard penises being forced in and out of hot silky vaginas. Oh and the sounds. All four of them making depraved animal sounds." She imitated the sounds, not too loud or too strong. He liked his sex talk to be gentle and soft, with no harsh graphic words. Once before she had tried to be more explicit but it turned him off and he hung up immediately. She lost money that night. Money she needed for drugs. The cocaine she needed daily to get her through the strain of her perverse trade.

The Priest moaned softly to himself. The images she painted with her words made his groan ache. He didn't touch himself in the booth. Instead, he enjoyed the throbbing, agonizing built up that later lead to immense pain. He would not relieve himself of the pain by masturbating. He considered his pain to be a punishment from God for making the calls and vowed to endure the discipline. Slightly hanging his head, he closed his eyes again. "Tell me more child. Tell me more."

"Sometimes I wonder about the other types of men that lived in Sodom and Gomorrah. You know the ones that raised farm animals, like sheep?"

Angry and abrupt, he yelled, "No animals."

"No, no. I meant the sheepskins. They must have used them to fornicate on." She managed a recovery by talking quickly. "I mean young farm boys could enjoy the feel of the fleece against their naked flesh. It would cushion the boy's knees while he took the other boy into his mouth. Dirty boys that lived in Sodom performing obscene acts on each other. Oh, Father, I imagine the one boy laying on his stomach while the older, larger boy holds him down as he pushes himself into the weaker boy. The smaller boy begs him to stop because it's his first time and it hurts so much."

"No. Stop." His words were sharp, "Women, only women. Speak more...more of the whores." The pressure was building in him. He gripped onto the phone itself for balance. "More filthy, slutty whores."

"Look." Richard pointed to the screen.

"Whoa." Brogan grinned.

"In the dirty filthy steam rooms, men would lay down their money for wine and cheap women. Painted whores who would do anything perverted for money or cheap wine. The whores would..."

There was a knock on the booth door. "Father. Are you all right?"

Startled, he jerked around violently. Panic rushed through his body so rapidly he didn't hear the credit card dropped to the floor. He opened his eyes to find a middle-aged bawled man staring at him. Questions poured through the priest's mind; 'How long had he been standing there? Did he hear anything that he said to Jezebel? Was he from his own congregation? No, he wasn't. He in his head he thanked the Good Lord, he was a stranger.'

The man was now holding half of the door open. "Is everything all right, Father? You've been standing here for quite a while now and haven't moved at all. You're breathing is erratic too. Are you ill? Do you need help?"

The priest could hear Jezebel asking him if he wanted her to continue. He calmly spoke to her, "No that will be all for this evening. Thank you for your words of inspiration. They have been enlightening. God be with you." Casually he hung up the receiver and stepped out of the booth. Mentally pulled himself together. Now he would have to formulate a lie to cover up the situation. Another sin. "No, my son, I'm fine. I've been listening to sermons written by other priests and ministers. Sometimes even I need stimulation...to assist me in preparing my own sermons. New topics. It's like research." He forced a saintly grin.

"You were breathing so hard and your face was turning red. I thought you were having a heart attack."

"No, no, I'm fine." He gestured with his hands toward the booth, "Did you wish to use the phone?"

"Yes Father, I would. I always call my wife before going home. You know, to see if we need anything. We always seem to be out of milk or bread or something like that."

"Then I'll leave you. Have yourself a pleasant evening and God's Blessings." Pretending as though there was nothing wrong, he strolled away slowly, mentally squashing his erection. He walked behind the van and disappeared into the shadows.

Inside the booth, the man pulled a handful of change from his pocket. As he held his hand open to the dim light and searched for a quarter, something beyond his hand caught his eye. A small golden rectangle on the floor. Realizing it was a credit card; he picked it up and read the name, Mr. Paul Smitherson. Checking his watch, he decided to call the credit card company after he called home. Once again, he fished out the change from his pocket and searched for two quarters. He popped one in and dialed.

"Hello?"

"Hi Honey, how's your night?"

"Good. Supper's in the oven waiting for you. Roasted chicken with herbed potatoes." The monitor showed the sour face he made.

"Is there anything you need from the store?"

"Yeah, O. J. for breakfast."

"Okay, um...listen I found a credit card on the floor in here and I'm gonna call the card company to see what I should do with it. So I maybe a little bit longer, okay?"

"Yeah. You tell me all about it when you get home okay? Love ya, bye."

"Ya, Bye." He clicked the phone down with his finger and put the other quarter in. Flipping over the card he entered the 1-800 numbers.

"You have reached Coastline Credit. To serve you better please select one of the following options. To report a stolen or lost credit card, please press one. To inquire..."

He pressed the one key.

"Thank you. All of our service representatives are currently busy, please hold and someone will be pleased to assist you as soon as possible." He sang along with the catchy music while he waited.

"Good evening. My name is Susan, how may I help you?"

"Well, I've found one of your credit cards on the floor of this phone booth and I'm not sure what to do with it."

"And the card is not yours sir?"

"No, like I said I found it." He rolled his eyes at her inane question.

"Oh yes. What I need from you sir is the card number please." He read off the numbers and she read them back for verification. "Perfect sir. That card has now been canceled. I will also have another one of our service representatives call the cardholder to let them know their card has been found and has been canceled. Now the next thing we need from you sir is to have you destroy the card. Please cut the card through the magnetic strip and then into six pieces or more. Then dispose of it into a secure garbage receptacle."

"No problem. I'll do that right away."

"Do you have any further questions, sir?"

"No, I'm good."

"Sir, on behalf of Coastline Credit, we'd like to thank you for taking the time to report this lost card."

"You're welcome and good evening to you."

"Have a good evening sir."

He hung up the receiver and stared at the card. "Where in the hell I'm I going to find a pair of scissors at this time of night?" He shrugged his shoulders and stuffed it in his pocket. Leaving the booth behind, he headed around the corner to King's Variety Store.

Brogan pointed with his nose, "Look who's back?"

Once the husband was out of sight, the priest ran to the booth and searched its floor. "No. No. Where's my card? My Jezebel. No. She's gone." It was gone. He leaned back against the booth's wall and slid to the dirty floor. He made no sounds but slumped in silence.

"Hot babe, ten o'clock." Brogan found the priest's grief hard to believe. He decided to lighten the mood by giving a blow by blow play, "Welcome to tonight's main event." He announced it into his pen, his imaginary microphone. "Yes folks, it's a race for disgrace."

Richard was on the priest's side, "Come on you idiot, get up before she gets here."

"Oh fans, she's almost to the curb."

"Get up. Get up!" Richard couldn't stand it. He pushed his chair to the steering wheel and honked the horn.

"He's opening his eyes...she's slowing down...he sees her...she's stopping...she's looking in her purse...he's out the door...she's going for the booth...they nod...oh, oh...and he's outta here. The crowd goes wild." He made that phony stadium crowd sound with his cupped hands.

"Fuck Brogan, you're killing me."

"Yeah, yeah. Shut up. She's dialing."

"Anderson Answering Service, Cindy speaking. How may I direct your call this evening?"

"Yes, my name is Alice Dale and I have an unusual request. I need to leave a message on my own answering service. You see, I'm a writer and I've forgotten to bring my notepad with me. And I've got all these great ideas I need to jot down right away before I forget them. So I was thinking I could leave them on my service and copy them out when I get home."

"That's no problem at all Miss Dale." There was click sound on the line, "And ma'am it's not that unusual of a request. We do the same thing for our other clients all the time."

Her voice was filled with self-amusement, "Really? You mean I'm not really that eccentric after all?"

"No. It's a common request. I'll put you through now. Thank you for calling Anderson's Answering Service. Have a pleasant evening."

The phone briefly hummed, then her voice announcement came on. "You have reached the answering service of the wonderful Alice Dale. Please leave your name, then your number and a brief but happy message. Thanks." It was followed by a long beep and then the silent recording time. She began to dictate her thoughts. "Alice, change that ridiculous opening statement, it is stupid. Where do I start? Okay, we met for coffee around seven o'clock. He looked really good. He wasn't wearing his work clothes, but a clean pair of jeans and a fresh T-shirt. They weren't even faded or stained. He had shaved. I hadn't seen him shaven in a long while. I had always wondered what his rough beard stubble would feel like against my delicate flesh. But today the skin on his face looked so soft, so clean and so smooth; I wanted to stroke it lightly with my fingertips, savoring the sensations. I wanted to place my pale cheek next to his. I wanted, no needed to press my lips on that soft dark handsome face again and again. To savour that smooth heat against my lips. I wanted him to return that kiss, over and over. My crotch turned to fire. My heart raced and I started to breathe heavily. It's been years since I've felt this way, all these yearns tumbling at me at once. And his eyes, they are so green-blue, like looking into a deep Bermuda sea, calm and stormy at the same time. 'A sexual rush' that's the words I want. His lips. Oh, I want to kiss those lips. No, I want to devour those lips, his mouth, the very air he breathes. Um...that's a little strange Alice, reword that. You can do better. Think, think, think. Oh, oh, his jawline," After a long contemplative sigh, her voice went from excited to soft and sultry. "Oh yeah, his jawline.

Um...I want to kiss his lips and nibble up along his long strong jaw, ending at his ear where I'd whisper, 'I want you to f ...'" Loud beeps announced the end of the recording space.

"Shit, shit, shit. Not now, I'm just getting going. Crap!" She hung up the phone, put in another quarter and called back immediately.

"Anderson Answering Service, Cindy speaking. How may I direct your call this evening?"

"Hi Cindy, its Alice Dale again. I need you to put me through to my account again. I didn't get it all in. I ran out of time. And Cindy, is there any way to lengthen my recording time?"

"I'm sorry ma'am, I don't have the authority to do that. If you call the office tomorrow, I'm sure they can arrange that change for you."

"But damn it all, that won't help me tonight," she realized she was yelling at Cindy. "Oh, it's not your fault, is it? I'm really sorry. Oh well, don't sweat the small stuff, that's what I always say. " In the booth, she shrugged her shoulders. "Please put me through to my account then. And thank you for your help, Cindy." Next came her annoying message and the long beep. "There we were sitting at a table in the middle of the restaurant surrounded by at least thirty other people and he shows me how to roll back the knob on my ancient computer monitor. He put his hand palm up in front of me and with his middle finger starts stroking his fingertip back and forth imitating how to roll it. That motion sent a shiver down to my crotch again. It looked so much like he was stroking me I couldn't help but imagine him actually doing that to me.

Another sexual rush. I think I even blushed a little." She paused to orchestrate her thoughts. "I also noticed how rough his hands were. I instantly wondered what it would feel like to have his rough hands on my soft warm breasts. Another sexual rush. I pulled myself out of it and tried to concentrate on what he was saying but my eyes kept betraying me by glancing at his hands. He turned to thank the waitress for the coffee refill and I noticed that little tuft of grey hair at the back of his hairline. I wondered what it would be like to nibble right there at that spot on the nape of his neck. How would he react to my ravaging nibbles? With deep manly moans or silently indulging in the moment? What would he do next? Let me lead the way? Or turn around to repay my ki ..." beep, beep, beep, beep.

She slammed down the phone. "Fuck, fuck, fuck. I hate this. Time to get back to the loft and write these all down before I forget the sensations." She was still talking to herself when she walked out of range from the microphone. Brogan smiled to himself as he recognized the writer's head bobbing of mentally placing ideas in order. She stopped dead, pierced the air with her finger, and yelled, "That's it!" She spun around and headed straight back into the booth. In went her quarter. Her finger bounded out the numbers again.

"Anderson Answering Service, Cindy speaking. How may I direct your call this evening?"

"Cindy, its Alice Dale again. I need my account again."

"That's no problem, Miss Dale. I'll put you through right away."

"Please call me Alice and thank you."

"Okay...Alice, here you go. This time I'll bypass your opening message."

"You can do that? Thank goodness for small mercies." She heard the long beep and began dictating her thoughts. "I dropped my napkin on the floor when we stood up to leave. It fell on the floor at his feet. I crouched down to pick it up, seeing that his crotch was level to and directly in front of my face. Holy cow, he's packed. Big packed. His jeans cupped him tightly. Oh, how I want to know what's behind that zipper. Is it long and slim or short and thick? How will it look? How will it taste? Will it fill my mouth? Will it fill me? My hand tightened against itself in anticipation of its texture and heat.

My mouth fell open in the few seconds that I admired his jeans. I pulled myself out of that visionary moment only to realize he was looking down at me. Not lifting my head, I looked up at him with my eyes. My mind registered that this is what it would look like if I had him with my mouth. I stored that image in my memory for later. Bath time, bedtime, a time of self-indulgence. His eyes met mine for only a split second. To my surprise, I realized he must have been thinking the same thing. With a wicked twinkle in my eyes, I pulled away from his gaze and slowly lowered them straight ahead. There it was again, his deliciously zippered package. I closed my eyes and tried to think again, to breathe again.

"I slowly stood up and put the napkin on the table making the eye connection again. He stepped into me as though he was about to make his move, finally kissing me. Unfortunately, that's when Taylor yelled out his name and waved us over. The asshole ruined everything. As the two men talked, my mind wandered back to the image I had tucked away. I smiled politely at their conversation, all the while I was removing his jeans over and over again, each time in a different way. Soft, gentle, slow, caressing. Next greedy, hungry, animalistic. In my head, I could see him look down on me with his intense green eyes." She heard a noise on the line. "What was that? Is there someone there? Who's listening in?" Her face went sour, "Cindy, are you listening on the line?" She waited patiently for a response.

A meek voice came on the line, "Yes ma'am."

"This is a private call. You have no right listening in.," she snarled.

"Yes, ma'am. I know that ma'am."

"Why are you doing this?"

"Um...because I'm bored," she added quickly.

"Bored?"

"Yes, ma'am. This job is so boring. It's all I can do to stay awake."

"Shame on you! I should report you to your boss."

"No don't. Please don't, I'll get fired. I'm a single mom with two boys. Please don't tell my boss, please."

"Cindy, have you ever done this before?"

"No, ma'am. Never."

Her writer's curiosity took over, "So why did you do it this time?"

"Because I'm a big fan of yours," she sheepishly confessed.

Out of shock, she questioned her, "How did you know it was me? I write under a pseudonym."

"Like I said ma'am, I'm a really big fan. I read your biography in one of my old writer's magazine so I know your real name."

"I guess you really are if you remember that particular piece of information about me. That was over fourteen years ago and the only time my real name to be printed. It was also against my wishes. A mistake I'll never make again."

"Ma'am I'm sorry but I swear, I wasn't trying to be mean. It's such a thrill to hear you drafting a real live storyline. I can't wait to tell my mother about this. She's a huge fan too."

Her voice turned angry, "You'll do no such thing. My storyline is part of my business. You'll tell no one or I WILL get you fired."

She sounded surprised and relieved, "You mean you're not going tell my boss?"

"No, I am not. But no more listening. You got that?" The latter was a direct order.

"Yes, ma'am. You've got my word ma'am. I swear!"

Her voice went soft and friendly again, "One more thing, I told you to call me Alice. "The title of Ma'am makes me feel old and I'm not old. I'm too damn young to be called Ma'am."

"Okay...Alice." She giggled with delight at being given the privilege of her friendship.

"And I've got one more question. Do you really like this storyline?"

Cindy let out a long-drawn whistle. "It's gonna be a hot one. Even better than your latest book. I'm reading it right now. Which by the way, I can't put down. Um...but Alice, if the guy is such a hunk why are you alone? Shouldn't you two be in bed by now?"

"We haven't been on an official date yet and besides, he works nights."

"Oh, that's too bad."

"Not really, I prefer to write at night. It's perfect."

"That's kinda funny. I'll be reading your book later tonight. It's the only quiet time I get. Your books are so gloriously obsessive."

Obsessive, she liked that description. "Thank you. I'm glad you enjoy my work. Okay Cindy, put me back on so I can get this storyline down tonight. And no listening, you hear me."

"Yes, ma'am. Sorry, I mean, Alice," she giggled again. "I'll put you through. And good luck with the new book. I can't wait to read it. Have a good night...Alice."

She heard the long beep again and Cindy's click. "Now, where was I? Oh yeah, his T-shirt. Um...tonight he was wearing a very tight dark blue T-shirt. It clung to his well-defined muscles. His hard nibbles erupted through the soft, smooth material. Oh, how I wanted to lick those tiny rigid morsels. I wondered what is under that shirt. Are there any scars? Maybe from an accident on his motorcycle. Tattoos? Tattoos from his reckless youth. Is his chest covered with soft dark kinky hair? Is his stomach taut with muscles?" She couldn't concentrate, the words Cindy had said kept rolling around in her head. She gave in to them. "Note. Sent a signed copy of this book to Cindy at Anderson's service, she'll get a major kick out of it. Where was I again? Shirt ...um...um...oh crap it's gone. Shit!" She hung up the phone. Checking her watch, she continued to talk to herself. "I can be back at the loft in fifteen minutes and it'll take ten minutes to type it up on the computer. Then it's bedtime. Oh my, my, I'll have sweet dreams tonight."

She left the booth with a frown of deep concentration and muttered to herself. Her finger placed her thoughts in sequence on an imaginary 'air list' as she disappeared around the corner.

Richard shook his head, "Wow, she's a weird one. Wild but weird."

"She not weird, she's a writer. We're all like that." Brogan said sheepishly.

"Oh yeah forget you write stuff. You publish anything yet?"

"No. And that's not why I do it anyway. It relaxes me. It helps me keep my mind sharp."

Richard burst out laughing, "Oh yeah, that's working out well. You're about as sharp as a used writer's pencil. Dull and pointless."

"Shut up, Dick Head."

From the alleyway came a lady dressed in a pale blue pantsuit. It was evident that she was in a determined mood. Each step was precisely planted. Her navy slingback pumps clicked in the microphone as she closed in on the booth. The bangles on her wrist tinkled noisily as she reached for the receiver. Richard winched with the sharp pain before he had a chance to turn down his earphones. As before, Brogan focussed on the shoes and grinned to himself. She was already holding the two quarters in her hand when she slipped one of them into the phone. She pushed the buttons carefully, trying not to damage her extra-long, well-manicured nails. The phone rang four times.

"Hello?"

"Hi, Mom."

"Hi, Nelva. It's been a while since I've heard from you. How's the new job going?"

"It's great! I absolutely love it! I mean, who knew? Me, a fashion model? I'm still pinching myself to make sure it's really happening." It was difficult to keep her voice perky. She hated deceiving her mother that way.

"Have you been getting more work lately?" She had learned not to ask too many questions. If she pried too much it seemed to upset Nelva and she would claim she needed to go.

"Almost every day. I model every chance I get. You see Mom, when models start out they don't get paid much. Until they make themselves a name. Once I have established my reputation as a top new model, I can start to demand better contracts and more money."

"Are you making better money yet?" She was worried about her daughter's current financial situation.

"No, I'm still too new. My name hasn't gotten out yet. Soon though, real soon. I can feel it." When the big money started to come in, she would tell her mother how she had actually earned it. Until then she would keep the truth about her career to herself.

"So how are you money wise? Do you need money or anything?"

"Nope, I'm great. Just got paid yesterday. Rent and all my bills are paid." One and half thousand for one week's work wasn't bad at all. "In fact, I'm headed out to get groceries right now. Mom, I'm fine, so stop fretting."

"Yeah. I just worry that's all."

"So stop. Mom, the city isn't going to swallow me up or anything. I'm fine. I've got a respectable job with a great agent who takes good care of me. So relax. It's all good here. Promise." She made the sign of the cross hoping it would lessen the sin of lying to the woman who gave birth to her.

"Well okay. But remember, I'm your mother and it's my job to worry too much."

"Yeah, I know. Mom, I've got to go. I've got just enough time to pick up groceries before I'm due back at the Agency."

"But it's so late at night?"

She winced as she lied to her again, "It's a night shoot."

"Oh, sounds interesting. What company are you modeling for?"

That was the question she didn't want to answer. That was too big of a lie. She couldn't do it. She needed to avoid the question so she what she always did, she cut the call short. "I call you next week, okay?"

"Okay." Her mother was obviously disappointed.

"Love ya...and stop worrying. Everything is good here!"

"Okay, okay. Love ya. Bye."

"Bye Mom. Love you too." Her guilt weighed heavy on her heart, she told herself she would feel guilty later. But she right then she had something more important to do. She hung up the receiver and with the other coin placed her next call. Her pleasant expression changed to hard and cold as the phone rang.

"Back Stage Entertainment."

"I want to talk to Rene."

"I'll put you through." She was put on hold.

"Rene here. What's up?"

"It's me, Nevada. And I'm pissed. Listen here, you prick, where the fuck is my extra money for the anal job? You told me I'd get an extra $300 for that. Where the fuck is it?" She wasn't talking, she was beyond angry, she was yelling at high-speed.

"Slow down girly. Slow down!"

"Slow down my ass. I did the job. Now, where's my extra cash?"

"No, no. You've got it all wrong. I said I'd pay you an extra $300 for a double-action not just an anal."

"There no fuckin' way I'd do a double for a lousy $300. You pay Blossom $800 for a double. Why in the hell would I...?"

He cut her off, "Blossom's got a famous name that sells tapes. You don't. When you've got lots of fans following you, I'll pay you that $800 plus a hell of a lot more."

"You rotten lying little fuck! You said $300 and there's nothing extra on my pay. I want my money for that anal job or I walk."

"Walk where?" He was calling her on her threat, "And where do you think you're gonna go?"

"To Big John's. That's where."

He went silent. Big John was his main competition and he would pay top dollar for a babe like Nevada. Rene had big plans for her. With her beauty and skills, he would be rich in no time. He had dreams of buying himself a house in Hawaii and her talents were going to make him the money that paid for it. "Big John, eh? You've been talking to Big John?"

She heard the worry in his voice. Hostile and hard, she snapped, "Yep."

He tried to hide his nervousness, "And what did he tell you?"

"Well for starters, that you have a habit of promising big money and you never pay up. You've been cheating girls for years. Sound familiar? And what about the HIV tests? Is it true that instead of actually taking the blood samples to be tested, you throw them out and pocket our money?"

"That's bull shit! That's a total lie!" Mentally he asked himself, 'How did she find out about that little scam?' He would have to look into that later.

"Well one phone call will straighten that mystery up, wouldn't it?" Now she was getting smug, "Wait 'til the other find out about this?"

"Hey! Now hang on a God darn minute, Leave everybody else out of it. This is between you and me. You got that?" He was almost threatening her.

Her one word was delivered sharply, "Depends."

There was a nervous pause before he asked, "Depends? Depends on what?"

"Depends on what you're gonna pay me now?"

"Pay you now? What do you mean?" He was playing possum to see what she was going to demand.

But she wasn't buying into it. "Well let's see. Big John offered me a contract. A real contract. In fact, he suggested I take it to my lawyer so to have it looked over. My lawyer agreed that it's very lucrative and completely legitimate. He said I should take it." By the grin on her face and the confident way she conveyed it, she was obviously enjoyed that part.

With that he turned hostile, "If it's so damned great, why in the hell are you bitching' at me about it? Take the damn thing. See if I care."

This was the reason she called in the first place. "You know, you're right. Why did I waste my quarter on an asshole like you? You're a cheap loser with a second-rate loser company. Once everyone hears about the HIV tests, your business is done. See ya LOSER!" She slammed down the phone hard. "I'm free. I'm free." She did a little victory dance inside the booth. "I'm free. Here comes the big money. The big money I deserve. Goodbye Nevada. Hello, Suzette - French Sex Goddess." She bounced away whistling, 'We're in the money'. As she passed by the lawyer's building, she caught a glimpse of herself in the black glossy window. She stopped to check her hair and clothing. After playing with her bangs and fluffing the back sections with her fingertips, she pondered her reflected image. For the first time in a long time, she was completely pleased with what she saw. She disappeared down the alleyway.

Brogan was grinning like a mad man. "I thought I recognized her face. That's Naughty Nevada. She's one of my favorite porn-star."

"Wait. You recognize her face? You mean you actually look at their faces?" Teasing Brogan was so easy.

"Shut up. I'm serious. Look at her. She's a natural beauty. She's got all the right curves, not too skinny. Look at those long legs and her breasts, there perfect. 'm damn sure they're real too."

"How in the hell can you tell that?"

"You know that Blossom chick she mentioned? Her tits are fake. They're too round and too firm. They don't sit right. Real breasts move differently. They shift to the s de when a chick lies down, they don't stick straight up l ke boulders. They bounce differently too, more...natural."

"Wow, you've really studied this, haven't you?" Richard was trying hard to sound genuine. "So...um...how much research did you do to achieve this scientific theory of yours? Was it tapes, magazine or real live women that enabled you to formulate this miraculous hypothesis? Did you work on it night and day? It must have been an extreme sacrifice for the good of all mankind."

Brogan's notebook ricocheted off his head. "Fuck you dick head!"

Richard final let himself go. He slid the notebook back to Brogan's side of the desk, a devious grin on his face. "How did her feet look? Are they natural too?"

Brogan's face went pale. Had his secret been found out? He decided to play innocent in case Richard hasn't discovered his fetish. "What are you talking about?"

"Come on man. I've known you for years. You're into feet. They turn your crank. What's wrong with that?"

"How? When did you...?"

"Relax already. Your secret's safe with me." He realized Brogan was turning ghostly white. "It's okay. So you're into feet. There are worse fetishes than feet."

He looked over his shoulder at Richard and bluntly announced, "Shoes."

"What?"

"Shoes. Not the feet. The shoes."

Richard's mouth fell open.

"Yeah, shoes." He turned back to face his monitor.

They both sat staring at their monitors for a long time before Richard broke the silence. "Just shoes?"

"No. Any kinda footwear really. Boots, sandals, high heels..."

His voice was a mixture of curiosity and amusement, "High-top running shoes?"

"Fuck you!" He reached for his notepad again.

Hands in front of his face for protection, "No, I'm serious. I'm really trying to understand it, okay? I understand horny guys and pictures of naked tied up women. But shoes? I don't get it."

"I'm not sure what it is or when t started. All I know is that one day in the fifth grade, I noticed Emma Lupin's new glossy black 'Mary Jane's' and my dick went rock hard. BOING!" he made his index finger go straight out and up.

"Wow, that young?"

Brogan nodded. "Yep. I was ten years old. There I was standing in the schoolyard staring at her shoes was a huge hard-on. It scared the shit out of me. I thought I was some kinda sick pervert. I hid it for years. Then when I was 17, I met Monica. She quietly informed me that she liked my studded biker boots and hinted that she enjoyed the exact same fetish. She introduced me to a whole new world of sexual experiences. She made me understand that I was unique, not sick. Eventually, I became comfortable with it and enjoyed it ever since."

"Um...can I ask a personal question? I mean, if you don't want to answer, that's okay."

He looked at him sideways, "What the hell. Let's hear it?"

"Girls. You found other girls who like this fetish too?" Brogan nodded. At that moment Richard's eyes grew big. Big with one revelation. "Your wife, did she know?"

Beaming, he turned his chair to face Richard. "Remember the Christmas party she wore that purple velvet dress that scooped way down low in the front."

"Oh ya. No offense, but you know I thought your wife was a knockout."

"Remember how all the guys tried to look down her top. Well, I was busy looking at her shoes. They were five-inch stilettos done in dark purple suede. Soft to stroke and touch. The heels were capped with gold metal tips, my favorite accessory. She had worn them that night just to please me." He sucked in air, "It was her secret Christmas present for me. Hot sexy shoes in a public place. Hedonistic as hell. You know, I still have them." He tossed his pen on the desk, "And no I don't still use them."

"Never said you did." Yet that too piqued Richard's curiosity. "What do you mean by use the? How exactly do you...um...enjoy footwear?"

"Well, it depends on the type of shoe. Now you take flip-flops, they fold in half and with the right lubrication, it feels just a pu..."

Richard instantly decided that he didn't want to know the details after all. "Look over there. "Tall, dark and handsome at two o'clock." As he pointed to the monitor, in his head he thanked God for the interruption.

On the east side of the block, a tall slim man limped down the sidewalk. His head was slumped down, his long brown hair cloaked his face from the camera. His pace sped up as he crosses the street to reach the booth. Raising his head, his hair fell back, revealing his face.

"I can't fuckin' believe it. It's Mitch. I'm gonna kill the fuckin' prick." Richard bolted for the van door but Brogan blocked him before he could get out.

"Where in the hell do you think you're going? You can't go out there. You'll blow our cover. Sit yourself down...right now." He tried to push Richard toward his chair, but Richard's bulky body didn't budge. "Look man, I feel the same way you do but there's nothing we can do tonight. We're stuck in here and that's that. So sit down." Brogan stepped into Richard's face, telling his partner he wasn't letting him out the van door. That made Richard back away from the door. Brogan eased the tension with a corrupt chuckle, "The best part. Now I know what the fuckin' shit looks like. That'll make it much easier for us to VISIT him next week." He gently placed his hand on Richard's shoulder and clutched it. "We'll get him, I swear on my wife's grave. That prick won't know what hit him, but he'll know why it hit him. I swear. Now sit down." When Richard didn't move, he added, "Please."

"Fuck! Yeah, you're right. Fuck n' rules." He plunked down in his chair. "Hurt him bad for me. Fuckin' prick."

"Already done, trust me." Brogan softened his voice. "You remember the Cecile Wheeler case. She was only 23. Her mother found her body in the kitchen. Her bastard boyfriend got all coked up and beat her to death. And for what? Forty bucks. A lousy forty fuckin' bucks." Rage replaced the softness. "Then the prick's rich Daddy got him a rich bastard lawyer and he turned himself in. Fucker knew he'd be treated like fuckin' royalty after that. We couldn't touch him." Hostility seeped into his narrowing eyes. "I couldn't do anything for that girl's mother, but I'm gonna make up for it this time around. Consider it done, Richie. Next week, I swear it. Right now we gotta do this job. Who knows, maybe the dumb shit will confess on tape for us."

"That would be entertaining, now wouldn't it?" Richard turned his attention to monitor and adjusted the recording equipment. "He's in. The rotten fuckin' shit."

Brogan intended to take plenty of footage of his face when he noticed something peculiar. Mitch's face was covered in

169

scratches, bruises, and dried blood. 'She fought back' was his only thought.

Mitch searched in his shirt pocket to find the quarter. A painful wince washed across his face. Sucking in air, he held onto his ribs while he lifted his arm to put the coin in. He listened to it fall through the machinery. He slowly punched out the numbers. It rang twice.

"Howdy?"

"Bob? It's me, Mitch."

"Oh Christ, where are ya now, boy? Y'all still at the hospital?" The older man spoke with a heavy southern accent. "Ya needs me to come fetch ya? Got the pickup all ready to go. Just say the word and I'm there."

"No, I'm fine. Really. Just a headache mostly. They let me out of the ER an hour ago. They said my head's fine but to stay awake for the next 24 hours just in case. I never thought she'd smash my skull into the wall. She's as mean as a bear when she gets wild like that. Hell, she tried to slice me with a butcherin' knife. Damn it all Bob, I tried real hard not to hurt her, but I've gotta protect myself too, don't I?" He blew out a deep breath to relieve the stress building inside, "The doctors at the hospital want me to see my own doctor in a week, to take out my stitches and to check my ribs."

"What the fuck?" Richard sat up straight in his chair.

"She's beating him by the sounds of it. I'm not believing it either. Let's play wait-and-see."

"She messed ya up real good this time, didn't she?" There was genuine concern in the older man's drawl. "Ya gotta get away from this gal. She ain't nothin' but a she-devil. She's been a spitfire since you meet her and she ain't gonna change. She's gonna hurt you bad someday. Mark my words boy. How hard was the crimpling' this time 'round? How many times ya gonna let her wallop you son?" He stopped himself before he yelled at Mitch.

"She got a problem okay? We'll handle it. She said she'd get help this time. She's trying to stay off the stuff but she slips once and awhile. That's all." He was lying. Inside he knew she would never be able to kick the habit. She lived for the heroine rush. Why couldn't she love him as much as she loved the heroine? He didn't know which hurt worst, the injuries she would give him or the pain of his heartbreaking.

"What'd that polecat do this time? Sell your TV again?"

"No. Last week she took some cash off the counter at the gas station. I confronted her about it and she went wild on me."

"She robbed the same gas station again? She's not real bright, is she?" Bob didn't use a euphemism. He called it what it was and used the word robbed.

"Thank God or she'd be dangerous." He smiled at the thought of Pam being a criminal. "Anyway, Chrissie saw her do it but didn't try to stop her. She called me instead. Chrissie's nice like that. When I got there, she played me the security tapes. There it was, plain as puddin'. Pam took it all right. All Chrissie said was she needed the money back so she could balance her cash tray or she'd be getting in trouble. I paid her the money Pam took and thanked her for her kindness. That's when she told me right out, that the next time Pam does it, she'd call the cops and pressing charges. No more breaks." Mitch chuckled, "And to beat all, just as she saying it, the cop that lives down the street from us walks in the damn door. It was a 'twilight zone' kinda moment." He took another deep breath. "That's what I was talking to Pam about it when she flipped out and started hittin' on me again. I thought it might help if we talked about...things."

"Come on boy. Stop joshin' yourself. She ain't gonna change. She's a lost soul that even our Good Lord can't save. Give her up boy. Move in with me for a spell. You'll get over her boy. You'll see." Bob's fatherly words came from the heart. If Bob could get him away from her, maybe he could make him see the truth about her. He needed protecting from a heroin addict before it destroyed him.

"Might be a good idea to take a break from her for a while. Just a couple of days. Maybe she'll be better by then."

"That's it, boy. You go get your belongings and hightail it over here. Ya know what I'm gonna say, don't ya? Get'er done, boy. Get'er done. Now say it for me."

"Get'er done." It was the crazy Houston family credo from back home but it still applied even here in the city. "Wow, that did kinda feel good. Get'er done."

"That's it, boy. Damn, you must be hungrier than a cougar at a chicken convention. I've got some good homemade stew, the beefy kind you liked back home. Tater dumpling sounds good to you too?"

"Kinda late at night but that would be great. Thanks, Bob."

"Hey, now wait a dang minute there boy. What's my name? Get it right."

"Oh Christ, not again." Mitch groaned.

"Ya got it. Bob's your Uncle." In the phone, he could Bob howling at his own joke. After twenty-six years Bob still thought that joke was funny.

"I'll see you shortly." He rolled his eyes, "Uncle Bob."

"Yep, see ya soon. And boy... if she's in there, don't go in. Come straight here. She'll try ta sweet talk ya again. See ya right soon Mitch." Uncle Bob hung up and the phone line buzzed.

Mitch slowly returned the receiver and leaned against the booth's walls. At the new angle, the camera picked up all the injuries on his face and body. His left eye was a swollen mass of black and blue. A large cut had been coarsely stitched together above the brow. His upper lip was fat and spilt. The cracked dried blood was still clinging in spots. Scratches from fingernails were everywhere on his face. He held his ribs tight as he quietly cried. He chanted the credo to himself, "Get'er done. Get'er done." His hands trembled with pain as he pushed the door open. Mitch limped away in the same heavyhearted manner that he had arrived in.

"Shit. She's a fuckin' junkie. I can't believe it. I was completely wrong. About her...and about him too." Richard sat there stunned. "How could I have missed it? I never miss shit like that. I guess, I just assumed it was the guy, 'cause it's always the guy. And I hate to say it, 'cause I thought I knew her. I should know better, I let my personal opinion cloud my judgment. Fuck!"

"Relax Richie. We've all seen it happened before. Husbands get beaten too and they never report it. It's like admitting to the world you're a wimp, a coward." The word coward bit back at Brogan. He had used that exact same word to describe Mitch hours before and now it had a totally different meaning. Like Richard, he was appalled by his own snap judgment of the situation. "Let's just pray that she got on that train and didn't change her mind. Worse scenario. She'll use the cash for drugs."

"Sally's gonna have a bird when I tell her."

Brogan decided to change the subject before Richard got too worked up and couldn't be calm down.

"Speaking of the family, how those little girls of yours?"

He was still kinda stunned by it all, "What? Oh...really good actually. Clare's in university up north. Delia's married and expecting her first baby."

"Man, I can't believe it. Seems to me that they were running the three-legged race not that long ago."

"Time is fleeting."

"Madness takes its toll." Brogan sang.

"What?"

"It's from The Rocky Horror Picture Show."

Richard shrugged his shoulders and shook his head at him.

"Never mind. It'd take too long to explain it all." He thought, 'Fatherhood must add years to a man life.' Even though there were only two years difference between them, Richard was a much older man than himself.

"Anyway, Clare is studying to become a lawyer." He candidly added, "Hopefully criminal law." It was not secret that he wanted one of his daughters to become a cop or close to it. A criminal lawyer would have to suffice.

"Ouch. That's gotta hurt the old wallet?"

"Nope. She's smart. Earned herself a scholarship for the first year and this summer she's interning for Mercer's office. She should earn enough to pay for most of next year. Besides, it'll look good on a job application to have an internship with a highly respected lawyer already under her belt. Yep, she's a smart one."

"Takes after Sally then?" His smirk disappeared quickly. This time it was Richard's notebook that flew across the van.

"Fuck you."

Brogan tossed it back. "Lighten up, buddy. It was just a joke."

"Do you have any idea what it's like being the husband of a scientist?" He slammed down the pad on his desk. "I get the gears all the time. She's smarter than him. Let Sally figure it out, she's the thinker in the family." He stabbed his pen into the pad. "Christ, my fuckin' IQ's 132. Doesn't it count? No. Last fall she was made head of her department. Big friggin' deal."

"Why's your face turning red. I thought envy was green."

"Shut up! Prick!"

Richard's jealousy of his wife was pissing Brogan off. "So your wife's smart. Damn it, Richard, you should be proud of Sally. The way she's proud of you. Christ, I hate guys like you."

"Guys like me?" He aggressively leaned forward in his chair. "What the hell that's supposed to mean?"

"Relax man," he waved his hands defensively, "You know you got a fantastic gal there. Kind, beautiful, sexy and smart to boot. Why can't you appreciate what you have? Guys like me would do almost anything to have a woman like that in our lives. Where's my Sally? When do I get a Sally?"

"You did. You had Maeve." Richard said it in a softened tone. He didn't want to bring up painful memories.

Brogan bobbed his head in agreement. "You're right there. Maeve was the finest." He swallowed hard. "Christ I sure miss her." He blew out a long slow breath trying to hold back his emotions. "Question is...are we only allowed one 'supreme woman' per lifetime? Will there be another?"

After a reflective pause, Richard softly added, "Honestly, I don't know what I'd do if I lost Sally."

He turned to face Richard with a sorrowed expression, "Surprisingly, you'd move on. Your life kinda gets back to normal. For me, the pain eased up and I started sleeping in the middle of the bed again." He sat quietly watching the monitor. "It was well over a year before I allowed myself to even look at another woman."

"But you started dating again, right? None of those ladies measure up? Another Maeve."

"Christ no. Not even close. Well except Lolita. She might have been the best of the lot." He punched the button on the keyboard with his finger, "And look how that turned out"

"I couldn't imagine dating at this age. Hell, I have a hard enough time understanding the three women I have in my life now, let alone a total stranger. Makes me nervous just thinking about it." His body shuttered a little.

"Yeah, try this one. The first time I had sex with another woman, I completely fell apart afterward. Cried like a baby. It felt...it felt like I was cheating on Maeve. Even though she was gone, I felt as though I was being unfaithful." He did a street sweep with the camera. "Nina was great about it. She held me until I was done bawling. I felt like an absolute idiot, but she said not to worry about it."

"Yikes. Talk about your awkward moments?"

"Yeah, but the next time was much better. Nina and me split up after about three weeks but she was exactly what I needed at the time though. She heped my ego along nicely." He chuckled, "When I finally got in the grove, poor Nina didn't know what hit her."

Brogan was getting too boastful and Richard had to put a stop to that. He missed Maeve too and he didn't like Brogan bragging about his new conquests that way. He knew exactly how to piss him off and put a stop to his cockiness. He wheeled his chair across the van floor and took Brogan's hand. "Thank you for SHARING your emotions with me, partner." He quoted the psychiatrist's manual, "As partners, we NEED to EXPRESS our feelings like this more often and DURING our shifts together."

"Dick head." Brogan shot him a brutal look and shook his hand free of his grasp.

"Love ya partner," and batted his blue eyes while grinning at him.

He finally smirked, "Love ya too." They both laughed at the ridiculous new police psych program.

"Did you read that piece of shit?" Brogan moved the camera down the street. "What a joke?"

"Yeah. When will the big guys learn to leave us little guys alone?"

Brogan couldn't leave it alone, he had to know exactly what had happened all though years ago. He swung his chair around to face Richard, "Yeah, like the time you got me in trouble."

There it was. With those words, the light tension that had lain between them all night sat solidly in the air.

He was hoping that Brogan wouldn't bring it up but inside he knew that it needed to be dealt with. "That was a different situation and you know it?"

Brogan sat face to face leaning into Richard. His heart was bounding as he tried not to get angry, staying in control. "Why did you run out on me like that? I thought you were my partner? My friend? Why did you turn on me?" He stared Richard in the eyes, searching for any sign of regret on his part.

Bewildered by Brogan's accusation, he snapped back, "What in the fuck are you talking about?"

"After the investigation, I thought you'd still be my partner. When Birdy told me you wanted to transfer to vice, I couldn't believe it. Just like that, you were gone."

"Wait." He leaned back with shock, "Birdy told you that I WANTED to transfer to vice. What a bastard?"

"Bastard?"

"That fuckin' bastard!" Richard angrily swung his chair back into place. "I didn't WANT to transfer. They MADE me transfer."

"I don't get it. Why would they make you transfer?" To avoid looking at the side of Richard's head, he swung himself around to watch the monitor.

"Because they said, you didn't want to work with me anymore." The last few words came out slow and strained with inner pain.

He wiped his head sideways to face Richard. "What?"

"Yep. They...Birdy...said you were beyond pissed off and didn't want to be my partner anymore."

Brogan cut him short, "That's total bull shit. Well, except for the pissed-off part." He let his protective wall down, letting everything spill out. "Fuck. You said it was a man with a handgun. I saw what I saw and fired. By the time I realized that he was only a kid, it was too fuckin' late." Brogan closed his eyes in disbelief. "Christ Richie, I shot a kid. I still see his shoulder all blown apart, his bloody face in the dirt." His voice cracked, 'He was only twelve years old."

He yelled at him. "Don't do that to yourself. It was my fault. Not yours." He was trying to make him mad. He wasn't going to let brogan start crying. Richard couldn't deal with that raw emotion from the other cop.

It worked. He started to get louder, "Now that total bullshit. I'm a trained cop. I should have taken a longer look. Christ, I should have looked for myself. You know the rule? 'Don't take anyone's word for it. Trust yourself.' It was ME. I fucked up."

"No. We both fucked up and that's not the only rule. The other rule is 'trust your partner like you trust yourself.' WE fucked up."

"I pulled the trigger." He started to yell while jamming his finger into his chest, "I was the one that got into trouble. I was the one that got investigated. Not you."

That accusation made Richard livid, "Now wait just a damned minute. I got in my fair share of the shit too. Birdy let those Internal bastards grill me for two days before they gave up."

"Aw, you poor little thing. Two whole days. They interrogated me for two fuckin' weeks." He furiously whipped his pen across the room. "Fuckin' Birdy didn't do a thing to stop them either."

"He tried." He said it firm and sharp.

"How do you know? How in the fuck do you know?"

"Scuttlebutt was Commander Stone sent down orders that this case was to be made as clean as possible. No lawsuits. That boy was the nephew of this town's biggest lawyer. A well-known Black activist. Think about it. Two white cops mistakenly shoot a black youth in an alley because they assumed the boy was a Black man that was trying to kill them. Shit, it could've gotten racially ugly. Birdy did everything he could without getting his own ass in a sling. I still say I should've told them right from the start I saw the kid first and made the original mistake."

His face soured, "Yeah, you made that perfectly clear that day at the station."

Neither one spoke as they sat reflecting. Richard broke the silence. "I don't blame you for hitting me. I fuckin' deserved it."

He growled back, "Well, you called me a liar."

"I didn't call you a liar. I said you made yourself out to be a liar. There's a difference. His finger tapped out his opinion on the desk, "All you had to do was tell them the truth. Then they wouldn't have questioned your judgment " His fist hammered the desk, "You're a good cop, Brogan. Don't ever doubt that. You're one of the best cops I've ever work with."

"They didn't think so." He ran his hands over his face, "Fuck, they made me take an eye exam. That's how humiliating it got. By the time they got through with me, I was so frustrated that...well, no wonder I blew up."

"I didn't help either, yelling at you in front of everyone." He grinned his childish at Brogan. "Longest list of names I ever called anyone

"Yeah, I don't think they've ever seen partners' fight like that before." His angry face light up in amusement. "Christ, it took almost everybody from that floor to break us apart." He snorted. "And by the way, that was the first time I ever cleared off a desk using a human body." He looked sideways at Brogan, "It must have hurt?"

"Not as much as that kick in the kidneys. Fuck you're a mean ass fighter."

"Force trained, street mean." He crossed his arms, "And if you recall I was trying to protect myself."

He nudged Brogan's memory. "Oh yeah, I forgot about that."

"I wasn't interested in getting a folding chair in the head. You're a mean bastard yourself."

"Remember Birdy?" They both chuckled at the same time.

"Fuck yeah! From Black to red in thirty seconds," Richard joked.

Brogan slapped the desktop, "I thought his head was going to pop off."

"The best part was when you swung at me, I ducked, and you hit Foreman instead. Landed a beauty."

Proudly roared, "Knocked him on his ass. Felt good too."

"That's probably why Birdy stuck you with him."

Brogan grumbled, "Yeah, but was it punishment for what I did or revenge for getting him in trouble with the upper Brass?"

"Knowing Birdy...both," Richard confirmed.

"Trust me. It was a punishment." He angrily swung the camera down the street. "A long, cruel punishment."

"Look, I should...no...WE should have told them the truth right from the start. We would have avoided the whole bad cop crap altogether."

"I wanted to keep you out of it, that's all."

"Bull shit!" Richard twisted in his chair to face him again. "You didn't want to admit that you weren't paying attention 'cause you were too damned hungover." He stabbed his thumb into his chest to emphasize exactly how he felt about Brogan's lack of professionalism on the job. He turned his face away. Brogan could see that his jaw was locked tight. Stubborn-anger was a trait of Richard that Brogan had learned to contend with. "And just to set the record straight, I never reported that fact and never will report it."

Brogan quietly sat formulating what he was going to say next. He chose his words carefully while Richard tapped his pen impatiently on his desk. "I know that was hard for you, not telling the complete truth. I know it goes against everything you believe in. You're a straight-up guy and you lied for me. Thank you for that." He let out a held breath. "I'm sorry I put you it that position."

"We were both in a jam. What's really pissing me off is that they play us against each other and it worked. We fell for it. We're cops for fuck sakes. We should have known better." Richard still faced the monitor, "And your welcome and you're forgiven. Under his breath, he muttered, "Asshole."

Brogan wasn't sure if he was serious about the asshole part or not. But a soon as Richard started snickering, he knew it was all right to relax and joke around. He grinned at him, "You're the asshole...asshole."

"But you're the bigger asshole, asshole." Richard gentle tossed back the pen back on Brogan's desk. "Partner." That was the word Brogan had been desperate to hear. The tight knot in his gut unraveled a bit.

He picked up the pen and waved it at him, using it a diversion, "Thanks." To him that one word - partner, meant all was forgiven and they were good again.

"By the way, what was that crap with Birdy back at the office?"

"You'll need to be more specific. Exactly which 'crap' were you talking about?"

"The 'No bull shit. That's an order.' crap."

"Oh, THAT crap." He chuckled to himself, "Last year I was on a stakeout with Edwards and I pulled one of my milder practical jokes on him. Bastard went whining to Birdy and I got a reprimand with a two-day unpaid vacation."

"Edwards, Edwards? Isn't he that super religious nut that transferred from up North?"

"Yep, AKA Pious Pete." Richard was grinning like crazy. "He'd been preaching to me all night and I had endured all bible-thumping I could take."

"Wait, he was preaching to you. Shit, you go to church every Sunday. What was the jerk's problem?"

"I cursed in his presence. Stupid idiot thought I should refrain from using the Lord's name as profanity around him. He went on and on about it. He wouldn't shut up when I asked him to, sooo...I shut him up myself."

"Oh boy. What did you do?" He was pretty sure he knew the answer but was curious to what he did.

He nodded his head as he cheerfully announced his tool of choice. "Duct tape. The other silver handcuffs."

Brogan's eyes went wide, "You didn't?"

"Yep." He was laughing so hard, he was having difficulty getting it out. "Taped his damned mouth shut too. It was so easy right after I taped him to the chair. It was quite peaceful for the rest of the night. In fact, it was the best shift I ever had." He leaned toward Brogan with a big sinister grin, "And I'm packing a fresh shiny roll so watch it buddy."

"In your dreams, Dick Head." He flipped him the bird, "Like to see you try asshole."

"Too much effort. Besides, I'm getting tired. Time for a power nap."

"Yeah. It's almost four o'clock and no one had made any calls in...what...thirty-five minutes. You look like hell old man. How long you wanna...Nap?"

"Oh, fifteen minutes should do it." Richard swung his feet up on the desk and slumped down in his chair.

"Fifteen minutes it is." He decided Richard needed a longer nap then he had asked for. In his head, he added forty-five minutes to the time on his watch.

Richard squirmed in his chair to get the right butt position, "Nighty, nighty lover boy."

"Christ, just go to sleep, ya asshole."

Seven

Richard shut his eyes and let out a heavy sigh. Within minutes he was wheezing softly like an old man in his favorite armchair. Brogan envied his effortless ability to sleep anywhere, anytime. It was a talent that he had never mastered himself. It wasn't uncommon for him to only get a ten-minute nap on his stakeouts, even in sedate times like it was that tonight. It was as quiet on the streets as it was in the van. Only an occasional late-night loner passed by the locked shops. SPOONS had shifted into full night mode as well. At one of the tables, Nick was playing solitaire and the cook was reading the newspaper that had been left behind earlier in the evening. After twenty minutes of staring into the monitor, Brogan's eyes began to feel heavy. In attempts to stay awake he reached in his bag for his sketchpad. Opening it to the last sketch he had created, he realized it was a fine line drawing of Lolita. She was nude.

He had never actually seen her naked but this was how he envisioned her long, lean body would look. His imagination had portrayed her lying on a bed, her long slender legs and curvy hips entangled in satin sheets of sapphire blue, her head resting upon a huge opulent pillow of the same intense color. Each lock of jet-black hair was placed exactly where he wanted them to be. It framed her angelic face and spilled downward to conceal her shapely breasts. His artistic skill made it appear as though her hair had lightly fallen into place just seconds before. A string of ruby beads clung to the nape of her neck, at its end a thick gold crucifix. It was his gift to her, representing the union of beauty and purity that he saw in her. Her Latin eyes held that fiery darkness that made him melt whenever they meet. It had taken him several tries to capture that vibrant sparkle that her eyes naturally held. Her sultry lips were glossy and slightly parted. In his mind, she was about to invite him to lie down beside her. This was his fantasy of her. An image filled with his desires. An image that no one could take away...until that night. The cold hard truth sliced into him. Lolita was in love with someone else and that someone else was a woman.

The sketch blurred as tears filled his eyes. He closed the sketchpad and emotionally let himself go. Quietly crying, his body trembled with the release of his heartbroken pain. The pad slipped from his hand and crashed to the floor. Richard stopped wheezing and stirred in his chair. Brogan, nearly terrified, watched him closely. If he woke up, he would see the sketch pad and ask to see what he had been working on. That would be too humiliating for him to handle. To his relief, Richard began to wheeze again. Gathering the pad together, he jammed it back into his bag.

Lifting his head, an odd image in the monitor caught his attention. A tiny brown dog with white patches wondered from signpost to signpost, sniffing here and there, each time marking his territory with a healthy squirt. Brogan wondered how the little dog could pee so many times. He was a small dog, so he had to have a small bladder? Where did it all come from? Realizing he was contemplating the function of a dog's bladder, he decided to occupy his time with something more productive—and not so absurd. Brogan checked his watch again. He would wake Richard in another thirty minutes, giving him even more time to sleep. Still bored, he reached for his other favorite portable hobby—writing. Paper and pencil had been his best friend when no one else had bothered.

Inside his bag, he shoved the sketchpad aside and pulled out a brown, leather-bound journal. He inhaled its earthy aroma. Its corners were mashed and frayed, its spine was broken from months of abuse. Opening the front cover, loose pages scattered across the desk. He gathered the papers together, making a single pile in front of him. The top page glared at him. It was filled with quickly scribbled descriptions of moments spent with Lolita. The agonizing stab of heartache pierced again. Mentally he read the rough-hewn entries.

'I touched her hand today. Her skin soft, warm and so tan. Does the rest of her body feel that luscious? I want to feel her body against mine. I want to hold her while she sleeps.'

'We passed each other in the hall. She smiled at me with her kissable lips. The scent of her filled the air as she walked by. I can still smell her in my memory. I need her.'

The pages turned liquid through his tears. Sucking in a deep breath, he stuffed the loose pages into the back of the book and as a little boy would, wiped away the tears with the flat of his hands. That's how he felt at that moment. Like a little boy, small and venerable. Damaged by the world, the harsh world of love.

He forced himself to breathe normally. To simply breathe at all. He switched the self-talk in his head. He told himself, he wasn't a little boy anymore. He was a man and men don't cry. "Damn it!" His curse split the silence of the van. Richard's mouth closed, stopping his wheezing. His hand slowly slipped down into his lap. Luckily, he remained dormant and his wheezing turned into a light snore. Inhaling another deep breath, Brogan blew it out gradually while mentally droning his mantra. 'Arms, knees, paws.'. In through the nose, out through the mouth, just as his anger management instructor had taught him. He was surprised at how those meditation lessons worked in times of stress. He continued to repeat the process over and over until the raw tensions in his chest vanished. Blowing out one last slow breath, he opened the journal to his last entry. Not remembering what he wrote over two weeks ago, he read the last paragraphs in attempts to refresh his train of thought.

A new subdivision was being built in the fields beside my Mother's house. Those fields were the playgrounds of my childhood. In the patches of sumac, we built the forts of brave warrior Indians and cowboys of the old west. Ostrich ferns were fashioned into arrows by trimming their foliage close to where the feathery leaves forked. Long poles from a young popular tree became spears and tomahawks consisted of a short thick stick, a flat rock, and bits of yarn stolen from my Mother's yarn basket. Many battles were fought, lost and won in those fields. Battlefields of youthful naive fun.

NARCTURNAL

The last house to be constructed was right next to my Mother's property line. On that lot stood the last remaining beechnut tree of an original group of three. As a child, those three trees were Mother Nature's jungle gym. We scaled the limbs of the century-old giant, pretending to be monkeys or mountain climbers. We tied ropes for swings. Carefully wedged boards became Captain seats for spaceships, schooners, and airplanes. On searing hot summer days, they provided the only air-conditioning we knew, gentle breezes blowing through cool shaded branches.

With penknives, initials were craved into soft smooth bark. Couples declared themselves promised for all to see. Later touching those scars evoked smiles and memories of true loves lost. We thought these trees would exist forever—beyond our eternity. But tomorrow, its body was to be slaughtered. Its limbs dismembered. Its severed pieces hauled away in the back of a truck. Tomorrow they would murder a living thing, ending the life of my century-old friend.

Where would my initials go? To be burnt in a beach bomb fire or the fireplace of some overpaid yuppie? It would hurt to see it disappear, to watch my youth destroyed in a matter of hours. I asked the man, 'Why can't you just leave it there?' All he said was, 'It's in the way of the bulldozer. We can't get around the damn thing. Its gotta go!' How could he be so callous about assassinating my memories—my childhood, my ancient friend? And what of the memories of the children yet to come? What gave him the right to decide if the tree mattered or not?

Richard snorted on a choking snore. His body jerked making him wake up abruptly. "What?" He coughed on his dry throat. "What happened? What time is it?"

"Well, it's about time you woke up. You old fart!"

He pulled himself upright in his chair. "How long have I been out?"

Brogan glanced at his watch, "An hour and seventeen minutes."

"For Christ sakes. I said to wake me up in fifteen minutes. Why'd you let me sleep so damn long?" He was half asleep and crabby.

Grinning like a devil. "Because you're an old fart, that's why?"

"Shit head. Now I won't be able to sleep when I get home? I told you how long I wanted to sleep. You always fuckin' do this."

"Still not a morning person, huh?" Brogan thought he would push his luck. "How does Sally put up with such a grumpy old fart every morning?"

"Fuck you!"

"Yeah, love you too partner."

"Shut up!"

"And as to answer your question. You didn't miss a thing. Well except for a dog that pissed on everything that didn't move. How do dogs do that? Where does all the urine come from?"

"What in the hell are you babbling about? Wait. We've got company." He sat closer to the edge of his seat and pushed his headset on.

A tall bony black woman with Swahili features stopped in front of the booth's doors. Walking around to the side and she leaned against the outer wall. She dug deep into her coat pocket for a package of cigarettes. Pulling a bright yellow lighter from her pants pocket, she lit the cigarette. In her hand, she turned and examined the lighter over and over while blowing out long streams of smoke.

It was Brogan's brand. "Man, I miss smoking." His mouth watered at the sight of the smoldering cigarette.

"You're kidding. You haven't smoked in what...gotta be ten years."

His voice held the glory of a victory that Richard, a non-smoker, couldn't relate to. "Twelve years next month."

"And you still miss it?"

"Yep. I've fought the cravings for all these twelve years. The desire never goes away. Right now my mouth is salivating for that cigarette she's smoking. I can almost taste it."

"That's one hell of an addiction." He adjusted the audio volume. "Sally would kill me or the girls if we started smoking. Her Dad passed away from cancer..."

Brogan broke in, "She's moving in."

Crushing the butt under her black arm boot, she went inside the booth. She slipped the coin into the phone. It rang six times before someone picked up.

"Hello." The person had obviously been asleep.

"Hi Bongani, it's me."

"Rudo? What time is it? Shit, it's five fifteen in the morning. Why are you calling so damn early?"

"He's done it again." Her voice was a combination of anger and disappointment.

"What?" He wasn't fully awake yet. "What time did he come in this time?"

"Come in? Oh no. Tonight he calls me from this house party to come get him because he was too damned drunk to walk home. So, like the idiot that I am, I get out of bed and go get him."

"Not again?" His mattress squeaked.

"Yep. Oh, it gets better ...or I mean, worse."

"Keep going." To him, their fights were either completely silly or thoroughly fascinating. This one sounded as though it was going to be entertaining.

"I get to this party and its all women in the house. Not one man in the bunch and he is so drunk, he can hardly stand up straight."

"What was he thinking? That's dangerous. With all those girl's he could have..." He stopped talking. He didn't want to add to his friend's worries.

"Apparently, he wasn't thinking. You know him. If there's booze there, he's there. Well at least until it's all gone." It hurt her to admit that last bit.

"Or until he can't walk straight anymore," Bongani added his own painful truth.

"Anyway, I walked in and every girl in the place looks at me like I was a fuckin' gargoyle or something. Half of them were irritated and the other half seemed disappointed that his wife showed up. It was like these girls were looking to score with him or something."

"That must have pissed you off?"

"Damned right it did. So I hauled his drunken ass out of there and headed home so I get some sleep. Then out of the blue, he starts crying and screaming, 'my life is shit. I'm no damn good, blah, blah, blah." She took a deep breath to stop her blood pressure from rising again. "Same old crap. From what he was bawling about, I guess he'd spend yet another night crying into his beer about the state of his life."

"What do you mean 'about the state of his life'? I thought it was his idea to stay home?"

"No. The only reason he's at home is because he's too fuckin' lazy to get a job."

"What about his depression? That's gotta make it difficult for him?" Bongani's sister was diagnosed with bipolar depression years earlier and he empathized with the distorted mental torment that manic/depression could put a person through on a daily basis.

"No, you've got it backwards. He's depressed because he IS staying home."

"I don't get it?"

"His depression is caused by the fact that he has nothing in his life to occupy his time. He spends hours worrying about pointless things. Like a microscopic pimple that no one could possibly see unless they stood inches from his face and he pointed it out to them. Fuck, it takes him an hour to make his Mohawk stand up straight. He doesn't do anything or go anywhere, except to the fuckin' Punk Pit. And house parties."

She started to yell, waving her other hand around. "He's losing it. Paranoia is the best way to describe it. He thinks everybody is talking about him all the time. It's like he thinks the whole world revolves around him. I spend hours on the phone every damn day trying to help him get his head on straight. He bugs me at work for Christ sake. It's driving me nuts."

"Shit, I didn't know he'd gotten that bad." The word paranoia caught his attention.

"And forget about looking for work. He got more excuses than a politician as to why he CAN'T get a job. He doesn't have a driver's license so he can't get a job out of town. Oh, and he won't get a licence because...well...each time we try, he conveniently gets one of his anxiety attacks and can't do it."

"He gets anxiety attacks?" This concerned Bongani because his sister suffers from them too. Anxiety attacks and paranoia are dangerous warning signs of severe depression.

"Yeah. What a load of crap that is! It's funny how he never gets anxiety attacks about going to beer bashes or a new bar."

"Never thought of that." He relaxed his concerns. If he was mentally deteriorating, he wouldn't be going anywhere. He couldn't function in that way.

"Get this, last week he tells me he doesn't want to work at a certain job in town because they're beneath him. He'd have to change his appearance and then he won't be happy and would end up quitting in three weeks anyway. Wish I had that choice." She fumbled with her cigarette pack, angrily jamming one in her mouth. "Yesterday's excuse was that he's too terrified to try something new because he might fail at it. He was fuckin' crying and everything. Boo-fuckin'-hoo."

"You're serious? Tough ass Mo Head, crying."

"Dead serious. Yeah, you should've heard him." She lit the cigarette. "In the meantime, I'm working at this shitty job I fuckin' hate. Christ now I'm giving him part of my paycheque and for what?"

He blurted out, "So he can drink it away." He felt bad for saying it out loud. "Sorry, I didn't mean it that way."

"Yes you did and you're right." She took a drag. "Let's face it, he spends almost every night down at The Pit, drinking and gambles with other guys while I bust my ass to cover the stack of fuckin' bills we have." She took another deep drag and blew it out hard. "Well, not anymore. He's got one month to get a job or move the fuck out!"

"Is that what you told him?"

"Not yet. Fuck, I just poured the drunken jerk into bed right before I came here. But when he wakes up and is clearheaded...wham, he's getting an ear full. No more bull shit. Get a job or get out!" She angrily flicked the ashes off the end of her cigarette with her third finger.

"You're serious this time, aren't you?" In his heart, he hoped she was going to do what she said she would so many times before.

"God damn right. Just because I'm married to him doesn't mean I have to put up with his bullshit. I've had enough." Bongani barely heard her whispered words, "and nobody calls me a danguro."

"Who called you a whore?" Shock turned to anger. She was a good person and no one had the right to call her that

"You heard that?"

"Who called you a whore? I'll kick their heads in! Whore is fighting word."

"Um, last week when I picked him up at the bar because it was raining?"

"Yeah."

"He was sitting at the far end of the big wooden bar. As I passed these two guys to where he was, the one leans over to the other guy and says, 'what a stupid danguro. She can't even make her husband stay home. What a fuckin' cheap whore.'"

Bongani felt bad for his friend, she didn't deserve the label or judgment. "Look, you know that's not true. You're not a whore. When it comes to being friends, you're the best. I'd want you beside me in any snarl I'd get into. You're one badass fighter, my friend." He tried his hardest to pump up his friend's ego. Being called a danguro was as bad as being called an unfit mother.

"Thanks." Rudo tossed the cigarette to the floor and bitterly stomped it out with the thick heel of her boot. "It doesn't matter. I have a feeling this is the beginning of the end for us anyway."

"Is it really that bad?"

"Bong, I don't want to spend the rest of my life looking at a man who needs constant reassurance. He's taking too much from me emotionally. I don't have the energy anymore. I'm exhausted from working extra shifts and keeping up with his midnight partying." The pause was brief, "I want out."

That's when it hit him. "It's you! You're the one who wants out and you're making him the heavy. You suck."

"No, this marriage sucks. It's repeatedly sucked. Fuck, look what he did right before we got married."

"You mean..." Bong said it cautiously, "...the other chick?"

Her voice turned harsh and bitter. "Yeah. That other chick."

"I thought you two worked that out?"

"How in the fuck do you work that out? He cheated on me. Down and dirty."

"But you weren't married yet?"

"Oh, so that makes it all right?" Incensed, she gripped the receiver harder. "I loved him. He loved me. Or so I thought. We were getting married in six months and what happens? Some slutty secretary nails my boyfriend in some motel room on a business trip and I'm supposed to be cool about it 'cause we weren't married yet." She kicked the wall. "How screwed up is your head?"

"Okay, okay. I get the point."

"No Bong, you don't." She grunted out her fury. "Imagine if I did that to him. All hell would've broken loose. He would have left me, fast and furious and I would've been labeled the town slut. But oh no, he gets to call it 'his one last fling' and everyone is all OK with it. Well, they forgot about me, didn't they?" Her high-pitched voice revealed her pain. "How could he do this to me? I've been good to him, haven't I Bong? Doesn't he get everything he needs? I know damn well that I've been loving toward him. The sex has always been great between us. What did I do wrong?" She held back the tears by holding her breath.

"You didn't do anything wrong. It happens, that's all. It just happens. When it happened to me, I know I didn't plan it, it just happened."

"Wait...you? You were unfaithful. When?" This revelation shocked her, Bongani was the most honest person that Rudo knew. That's why she had stayed his friend over all these years.

"It was before I met you. I was in college and had been going out with this girl for almost a year. Then this new girl shows up on campus. I loved Sarah. She was my soul mate. Tina was in almost all my classes. She was a knockout. All I remember is that one-minute Tina started flirting with me at the campus pub and the next minute, I'm in her bed, naked and incredibly confused. I never meant for it to happen...it just did. And yeah, Sarah did find out about Tina and yeah, she gave me the boot. Then Tina found out about Sarah and she wouldn't talk to me either. In fact, not one girl on campus came near me for a whole year." He let out a heavy breath, "The point is, it just happens sometimes."

"Fine, but that doesn't make this hurt any less."

'You're right. I never meant to hurt Sarah but I did and nothing I said or did could take away her pain. Shit, I had drinks with one of her friends last year. Susan said Sarah still doesn't trust men. He swallowed down the lump of guilt in his throat. "I did that. I'm responsible for fucking up every one of her future relationships. Ru, I never meant to hurt her and Mo Head never meant to hurt you either."

Rudo put her arm on top of the phone and noticed the time on her watch. "Holy Christ! I've got to go." She growled down in her throat, "'Cause I wouldn't want to be late for my fuckin' useless, brain dead job." She growled through clenched teeth, "I'll call you later."

"I'm here for you. We can go down by the lake and kick the ball around." That is where they went when they needed to get away from the world's bullshit. Soccer therapy, they called it.

"Yeah. Sounds good. Jambo, baby." She hung up the receiver and ran toward SPOONS. Nicky poured her an extra-large coffee. As if routine, Rudo scurried down the half-day lit alley, her steps turning into a light jog.

From the same alleyway came a short podgy lady in her early forties. Her pace was slightly staggered and slow.

Brogan chucked his pen towards his monitor, "Oh great. She's drunk," Brogan was in no mood to listen to a babbling drunk.

"I don't think she's been drinking." Richard shifted in his chair, "She looks like she tired. I kinda stagger like that when I'm truly exhausted."

"That's 'cause you're an old fart. And old farts get tired fast." His childish grin quickly faded when Richard's notebook dinged off the side of his head.

"Fuck you. And she ain't old or a fart, so shut up."

"Yeah, yeah. What-ev-er," Brogan tossed the notebook so that it slid flatly across his partner's desk. "She's going in, so...shut up yourself."

The lady pulled a quarter out of her upper jacket pocket and slipped it into the phone's slot. When she finished punching in the numbers, she closed her eyes and leaned her head against the glass wall. The phone only rang twice before someone picked up.

"Hello?" the female voice was sleepy and hushed.

"Hi. We're back." Her accent was an odd combination, slightly British, slightly southern.

"Your flight must have been late getting in."

"Yeah, we were stuck taxiing for over twelve minutes. Then there was a delay with our luggage. Something about a shortage of employees in the baggage department."

"I hate when that happens. How was our visit?" she didn't say funeral, it sounded too blunt and cold for this time of night.

"It was good, I guess. We saw all the relatives that we hadn't seen since Katie's wedding last spring."

"Isn't it always the way? We only see each other at weddings and funerals."

"You got that right. Aunt Angie and Uncle Steve say howdy."

"Say 'howdy' back when you talk to them again."

"Shall do. Cousin Jeremy got three kids and another one on the way. He's praying for a boy."

"That would be good, three girls in five years, no wonder he wants a boy."

"I bet Lori's praying for a boy too. So she can finally stop having babies." They both tittered.

"Dad's was hinting like crazy that the baby should be named after him if it's a boy and after Mom, if it's a girl."

"Well of course. It's the honorable thing to do. Carman is a beautiful name. It always suited your Mom. A beautiful name for a beautiful lady."

"Please don't go there. I'll start again and I don't want to cry anymore tonight. Silly me, I cried the whole car ride home. Blubbered like a baby."

"You are a baby. Her baby. It'll pass." She had lost her own mother six years before and understood the grieving process. She also knew she had to change the subject as her friend had requested. "Speaking of kids, did both of your kids show up?"

"Yep. Ivy was early and Arvon was late...as always. He lost weight. He's gotten slim again."

"And Ivy, what's she doing now?"

"She's a secretary at a law office. She says she loves the job and has finally found her niche. She looks good and so does her boyfriend."

"Boyfriend?" Her voice went high pitched with excitement. "That's new. When did that happen?"

"Just before Christmas apparently. And yes, it was a complete surprise to me too!"

"Do you approve?"

"Um...no piercing. Well, that I can see anyway."

"Is he good to her is what I mean? Please tell me he's better than that last guy."

"He treats her nice. But it might be because of the funeral." She swallowed hard and changed the subject again.

"He's a third-year law student. They met at the law firm where she works. He's interning there two days a week and when he's done school, he's got a job waiting for him."

"How's she holding up? Your Mom and her were super close."

"Yeah tell me about it. She was closer to her Grandmother than she was to me."

"Fanny relax, I was like that with my Grandma,"

She let out a low chuckle, "You know what she said to me as we were leaving the cemetery. "I guess I don't have to eat my crust anymore."

"What a weird thing to say."

"Frankly, I thought it was kind of amusing."

"Amusing?"

"Yeah. Of all the things she could have been thinking about at that moment, she remembered the 'toast fights' they use to have when she was little." She chuckled as she reminisced. "You see, Ivy would refuse to eat the crusts off her toast and Mom would demand that she eat them. Ivy would bellow NO and my Mom would command YES. And away they would go. At times, it was a mini world war in Mom's kitchen." She chuckled again, "Sometimes Mom won, sometimes Ivy won. But they'd always make up before we'd leave. I think she'll miss those fights the most."

"Okay, now it makes sense."

"Justine, I'm gonna go. I'm so dead dog tired, I'm about to drop."

"That's a good thing though. You'll go right to sleep when you climb in bed."

"I hope so. I can't think straight. My mind is racing like crazy."

"It'll stop," her voice was filled with reassuring experience.

"Yeah. I'm getting a take out for Alfie and me. I'm even too tired to make some breakfast. I'm going to get take away. I'll ring you later in the week when we've settled in."

"Okay Fanny, goodnight then."

"Night, Justine."

The phone buzzed as she hung up the receiver. She closed her eyes and hung her head down until her chin rested on her chest. She inhaled a jagged breath and let herself go. Her shoulders jerked with her sobbing. Richard turned down the volume until she lifted her head and was done crying. Angry with herself, she stomped her feet on the floor hard and grunted out, "Shit, stop it." She fumbled for a Kleenex and patted away the tears from her eyes and cheeks. After blowing her nose loudly, she inhaled deeply to gather her strength. With the same disheartened pace as she arrived with; she headed for SPOONS to place her takeaway order. She chatted with Nicky while she waited. She left with her order tucked under her arm, headed back down the alleyway and faded out of sight.

EIGHT

Brogan glanced at his watch. "Hot Damn Twenty minutes to go." He started to pack up his gear, stuffing it all inside his duffle bag.

In a wishful way, Richard added, "Wouldn't it be nice if the guys came early?" He stretched his arm up high and yawned at the same time.

"Wake up, you're dreaming again. I bet you they'll be late."

"You're on. Ten bucks says they're early."

Brogan poked in the air at him. "No. Fifty says they're late,"

"No, just ten. You've already pilfered fifty of my hard-earned dollars."

"No faith 'eh?" Again, the money was put on the desk.

Within a minute, the sedan pulled up in front of the lawyer's office.

Richard glanced at his watch, "Seven minutes early." He plucked the money off the desk and smugly announced, "Thank you."

"See. You should've bet more." Brogan shot at him.

They watched as Henderson and Foreman parked the sedan in the same spot they had shift before.

"Finally. I thought this fuckin' shift would never end!"

"You can say that again." Brogan wiped his hands over his weary eyes.

"I thought this shift..." Richard strikes again, "Gotcha."

"Shut up already." Brogan blew out a breath. "What a night? You know, mankind is really fuckin' screwed up. Everybody seems to be stealing, cheating or lying. I'm beginning to wonder if there are any decent, honest people left."

"Sure there is. Look at you and me. We're good people. What about the guy that found the credit card? And what about the friend of the Scottish lady? What was her name?"

"The friend?" Richard nodded. Brogan checked his notes, "Glenna."

"Yeah, her. She's good people. Uncle Bob too. Shit, he's putting himself right in the middle of a drug/domestic and we both know that can be a bad place to be. And what about Tim? The innocents of first love. That's always a good thing."

"Guess you're right." He focussed the camera on Henderson.

"When I first started as a cop, I felt exactly the same way you're feeling right now. It was Sally who sat me down and told me to knock it off. She pointed out the good things and good people in each case I was working on. Cases like the Peterson girl. Yeah, little Taylor was missing but do you remember all those people who came to search for her. More than five hundred volunteers showed up and hundreds of other people searched sheds and garage in their own neighborhoods. In fact, before we found the body, we knew exactly where she had been, right up until she disappeared. People cared enough to notice her in the first place and then took the time to call us with the info. Good people." Richard pulled the last tape out and put in a fresh one. "Unfortunately, that bastard Wallace was watching for her and pulled her into his van without a soul to see it. It was one of the worst child murders we'd ever seen in this city. Cut her up into pieces and hid her parts in the swamp two counties over. Sick fuck." Richard took a deep breath through his nose, controlling his anger and the tension it brought on. "Anyway, like I was saying, Sally still points out the good people when I forget to count them. She keeps me grounded."

There was a knock on the van door.

"What's the password?" Richard bellowed.

"Open the fuckin' door, Dick Head."

Brogan opened the door. "Yep, Dick Head, that's the password." Richard quickly stashed the last tape marked 'CASH' in his duffle bag.

"Jesus! You guys look like hell. I thought you guys usually slept all night." Through the window, he saw the cruiser door open. "Oh fuck, here comes Foreman. Shit, can't that guy do anything right? He's coming too soon."

"Nope." Richard grinned at him. "So what did you do to deserve him as your partner anyway?"

Henderson's face went deep red, "Shut up, Dick Head. You know damn well what I did."

"So how many cars in that parking lot did you smash into with your cruiser? Was it four or five?" Brogan's face stayed perfectly calm, making his joke even funnier.

"Three...and a corner mailbox." His face turned pink.

"Awe. Destroying federal property. Superb work." Unable to hold it in anymore, both Brogan and Richard lost it. Henderson gave them the finger before he opened the door for Foreman.

"What's so funny?" Foreman hated it when he walked into a bunch of guys laughing. It usually meant they were laughing at him.

"Nothing." They all went quiet.

"Fuck, I hate it when you guys do that." The guys started giggling again.

Richard was laughing so hard he almost couldn't get it out, "Yeah, we know. That's why we do it."

Foreman's face went cold but Henderson broke in before Foreman could let loose, "How was the night callers? Anything exciting?"

Brogan glanced at Richard. "Nope. Boring as hell."

"Yeah. A 'bring home orange juice' kinda night. Boring really."

Everybody looked at each other, then burst out laughing.

"Okay, spill it. Give us the dirt," Prodded Foreman.

Brogan flipped through his note pad, "Let's see, a porn star busting into bigger money but lying to Mom. A couple of alcohol-related domestics. A priest with a stolen credit card that fancies 1-900 numbers. Oh ya, Tony's a pot dealer."

"What? Tony's dealing from the pizza place?" They didn't even react to the priest's indiscretions.

"Yep. Once you get this perp, send in an undercover from narcotics and bust him. We got the deal on tape and I'm sure you'll get more today."

"Can do." He paused before asking, "Birdy said you called in for a tracker. What happened there?"

"We thought we had us battered woman, that needed protection but it turned out it was the husband that was the victim. She's an addict. Did you hear if she got on the train?"

"Bruce's report said she did." Henderson plunked his overly large butt in Richard's chair.

Richard shook his head with pity, "Poor parents. To have a junkie daughter in 'small-town-nowhere'. She's gonna be a hand full. It's gonna rip them apart."

Foreman farted—long and loud.

"Holy fuck! You asshole!" He held his nose making his voice nasal, "Christ you stink! Holy Garlic butt!"

"Sorry guys. It's the beans. I've gone vegan and beans are my main protein component." He looked at Henderson, "They make me fart. Sorry." He thought if he apologized in advance, Henderson might not be so bitchy the rest of the day.

"Oh, man. I'm sooo out of here." Brogan escaped out the door, sliding it closed right behind him.

Richard was too slow, "Shit, now I gotta breathe this toxic air for another ten minutes."

"Just ten. Consider yourself lucky. I've got a whole shift of Mr. Stinky Pants."

Foreman sat in front of the monitor, "Brogan's in the car."

"Screw procedure. I'm out of here." When Richard was halfway out the door, he turned back to look at Henderson, "See you later. Have fun with 'toxic boy'."

"Fuck you, Dick Head," Foreman yelled before the door slammed.

Brogan already had the sedan running when Richard climbed in, "To the office James." The sedan smoothly pulled away as they headed for the station. After a few blocks, Richard cracked the silence.

"Bro, I've got one question for ya?"

"Just one?"

"Ha, ha. Did you ever clear up those charges against you?" Richard's curiosity needed satisfying.

"Yep. And it only took three months and nineteen days. What a friggin' mess."

"So what happened anyway?"

"Burton confessed to having the drugs planted in my car."

"What? Why would he do that?"

"Turns out he thought I was the one that poisoned his dog."

"That's crazy. You, poison a police dog? Ludicrous."

"Tell me about it. Anyway, he set the whole thing up. Had some ex-con from down south break into my trunk the previous night before and put the cocaine in my first aid kit."

"Holy shit! What a rotten prick. That's dirty, even for him."

"Rich, I gotta tell you, when Burton and Norris pulled that bag of smack from my trunk, I thought I was a goner. If it wasn't for Birdy, I would have been hung by the balls."

"Yeah, I heard Birdy fought hard for ya."

"Face it. I owe him my life. Cops in prison don't stay healthy for very long." Brogan pulled into the police station. "Apparently, Burton and Norris went drinking one night and Burton got so shit faced, he started crowing to Norris about how he had set me up and how he was going to enjoy watching me finally go down for killing his dog. Norris turned him into Birdy the next morning. Said it wasn't right, what Burton was doing to me."

"Christ!"

"Yeah. They hauled Burton in but the prick wouldn't give it up. They questioned him for six fuckin' hours. By that time his girlfriend turned on him. She said he had asked her to be his alibi for that night. Seems, it's not a good idea to cheat on your girlfriend one week and then ask her to be your alibi the next. That's when he gave in and signed his confession." Brogan put the sedan in park. "They tell me that Birdy was the one that read him the charges and that he followed my case right through to the final sentencing. He told me he hated bad cops, especially ones on his force. All the charges against me were eventually dropped. Hell, I even got a 'we fucked up' letter, hand-delivered by Birdy himself. Still took over three months to get all the paperwork straighten out."

"Always takes forever."

"Burton lost everything. His shield, his pension and got the three years. Probably in protective custody."

"Poor shit. Good thing Norris was an honest cop and that he likes you. Could've been worse."

"Got that straight. Norris was great. He apologized right away. He told me he didn't believe I did it in the first place. His guts told him something wasn't right about the coke being hidden there in my first aid kit. Said he was suspicious why Burton insisted on getting into my trunk on that specific day and not handing it over to Internals. When Burton finally drunk babbled, Norris did everything he could to bring him down. Thank the Lord he did. My inquest was just starting when Burton started blabbing."

"The Lord works in mysterious ways. Doesn't She?"

"Yes, She sure does." The 'She' part was an inside joke between the two friends.

At last, Brogan felt comfortable enough to face Richard and ask, "Hey, you wanna go for breakfast after we get all this crap written up?"

"Holy fuck! You want me to spend MORE time with you? You're starting to sound like my wife."

"Oh, yeah. Sally."

Brogan's lusty grin almost pissed him off, but Richard let it fade away. "Brunch? That does sound good." He rubbed his tummy, "Yeah, I'd like that. What the hell, I'll call Sally and see if she can join us." He put on his best innocent face, "You know, she has this cousin Stacy. She's always wearing these super high-heeled shoes and kinda short skirts. Maybe you'd hit it off with her. I'll ask Sally to invite her along."

"Man, you haven't changed one damn bit. Richard the match-maker lives on."

"She's a blonde and she's got big boobs..."

The door to station house closed behind them.
Their shift had ended.

❖❖❖❖❖

other books
by
Kay D. Johnson

❖❖❖❖❖

Be sure
to look for
Kay's previous book,
Life on the Lawn

This is the story of four, lifelong, best friends - Fran, Pearl, Ruby and Violet, who attend the auction of Henry Phillips, the husband of their late-friend, Virginia. Henry, no longer able to take care of himself, he is forced to leave the farm life behind and retire into a nursing home. With his unwanted transition, comes the selling of his remaining possessions in a simple country action. Treasures and heirlooms that his greedy children do not care to inherit.

As the sale proceeds, these elderly Southern ladies share with each other the memories and adventures that are connected to many of the items up for auction. Tales of apple pies, lost lovers, and murder. Many of the local folk and neighbours gather to bid on the household items at hand, but it's Emmett, the worldly auctioneer, who is downright curious about the quiet outsider. Why is someone as sophisticated as him at a small town auction? Who is this unknown wealthy Frenchman? And why is he watching the four ladies so intently?

This is the story of one simple day,
at a not so simple auction.

Nitra Zupan faces the one crisis all writers' fear most, losing their entire hand written manuscript weeks before a looming deadline. Worse, she is unable to recapture the essences of her first page, the one she considers to be the most significant page of the entire book. After losing her manuscript to Mother Nature's wrath, she places an ad in the local newspaper offering a reward to have her pages returned to her.

Follow their tense adventure as they encounter the assortment of people who return the pages of her work, only to find them all, except for one. Neither, Nitra nor her house keeper, Wallace McPhee, is aware that the other has feelings that run deeper than their employer, employee relationship. That is, until they encounter the mysterious woman wearing gaudy red lipstick.

The comedic banter between Nitra and Wallace, along with the fast paced adventure, will bring you to the dramatic end of their search for Nitra's first page, the last page.

Be sure to
look for
Kay's previous book
MARKED
now on sale.

George Oscar Dack, a white warlock, is on the verge of shaking up his dull, predictable life. With the help of his sarcastic cat, Darius and a strange old woman, he conducts his experiment using precise elements and implements, to cast a spell upon a Canadian two dollar bill.

Writing his initials across the bill's front as part of the spell, it allows him to observe the bill's travels throughout the day, revealing what effects, either good or corrupt, it has on those who possess it, both young and old characters alike. Some have happy encounters, while others definitely do not.

Come join George and follow the bill's many adventures through his ordinary little town and discover the true connection between him and the old woman who enters into his life.

Be sure
to look for
Kay's previous book

In the hunt for ...
The Perfect Martini!

With a new job and a new life,
middle-aged Izzy Abbott finds herself
lonely and terribly bored.

Each evening, to spice up her life,
she disguises herself in an entirely new identity and visits a different
bar, looking for fun, men, and her version of a dirty dry martini
— her perfect martini.

Even though she is having a blast
on her nightly outings, the recent unsolved murder of a woman in the
city lingers in her mind while she party's. Should she feel secure or
watch out for her safety with a killer on the loose?

Meet the quirky patrons and peculiar bartenders she encounters in
the eclectic drinking establishments she visits.

Come join Izzy in
her zany adventures ... in the hunt for
... the perfect martini.

**Be sure
to look for
Kay's previous book
Bits Of Blue**

During a marital dispute between tormented Tess and her abusive husband, she finally gathers the courage to fight back for the first time. The result is the unintentional death of Morty Logan. Although it was an accident, Tess was convinced she would be blamed for his gruesome death if she called the authorities.

Determined to stay out of prison for the crime she did not commit, Tess hatched a plan to get rid of the dead body before the summer's heat wave gave her away.

Follow her internal struggles as she disposes of the body, bit by bit, using the one item she had plenty of — little blue zip bags, a sale item her controlling husband demanded she buy by the case.

While doing so, she must hide her true missions from the very nosy neighborhood senior and his friend, the meddlesome cop, both suspiciously watching every move she made.

No one knew what the timid Tess Logan had inside her tote bag as she walked about the city, looking for new places to leave her Bits of Blue

**Be sure
to look for
Kay's
previous Book**

Lovage

When single mom, Charlotte Thomas, moved into her new house, she had no idea that the man living across the street would take such offense to her scraping all the grass off her yard with a bulldozer. Against his friendly advice, she was determined to landscape her yard the way she wanted, no matter how much the good-looking Jack Lawson protested. Out came the grass — In went the stone, pea gravel and an abundance of vegetation, finally giving her lovage plant a permanent home.

But it was the elderly lady next door, along with her teenaged daughter, that quickly became very persistent matchmakers. Nicky and dear old Dottie were convinced that her mother needed a man to help Charlie create the garden of her dreams. A man that would eventually fall head over heels for the natural beauty of the stubborn blonde.

Come follow the romantic adventure of Charlotte and her neighbours, as they landscape her little wartime home. Who knows, you might learn some new gardening techniques along the way

Be sure
to look for
Kay's previous book

The Last Motel

Constantly on the run, Gabriel Carr was already exhausted when his headlights fell upon the neon sign that would dictate the next leg of his grueling escape. Through the heavy rain, he read, The Last Motel for 99 Miles. Finally able to elude the two mobsters hunting him down, he paid for a room to rest both his body and his mind. Depressed and drained of all energy to live, he took refuge inside the room, locking himself away from the world.

Gord, the motel's owner, knew right from the start that Gabriel would bring trouble to his peaceful motel. And when the stranger began spending time with Maizie, the secret love of Gord's life, he didn't like it one damned bit. Even so, he promised himself he would protect her and the others when that trouble did arrive.

It was Maizie, the housekeeper, that drew Gabriel out of his room and introduced him to her little town in Northern Ontario. His time spent with the beautiful and optimistic Maizie changed his mind about ending his life. Instead, he switched his focus on the mission started by his slain girlfriend, Heather.

Gabriel's new plans were going well — until the two hit men appeared, both prepared to eliminate Gabriel Carr, the only witness to the murder they committed. The end result being a dramatic gunfight and ending, no one could have predicted.

*Be sure
to look for
Kay's previous book*

*An Angel
Named
Topaz*

In the winter of 1977, Mickey Backus hires a Private Investigator to follow his wife Rosie, who he suspects is cheating on him. Not only did he want proof of the affair, he was also curious as to who was dumb enough to fool around with the wife of Belleville's notorious mobster.
Thank goodness, Mickey still had his beloved blue lined angel fish to talk to.

When Bernie, Mickey's right-hand man, also hires a Private Investigator, the competition heats up with everyone trying to get the photos the mobster wants. But when all is revealed by the Private Investigators, the identity of Rosie's lover both shocks and angers Mickey, setting off a chain of unexpected events that no one could have predicted, especially those of hookers and murder.

Come follow the bizarre string of episodes that entangle the even odder cast of characters — one being An Angel Named Topaz